THE SON OF YOUR FATHER'S CONCUBINE

(A COLLECTION OF SHORT STORIES)

'SEUN SALAMI

BOOKVINE®
publishability...

ISBN – 978-978-915-561-3

Published in Nigeria by
Bookvine
(Vine Media Services)
14, Adeshina Street, off Awolowo Way, Ikeja, Lagos.
Tel: +234 803 806 9951, +234 805 569 6965
Email: submissions@bookvineng.com
twitter: @bookvineng
Website: www.bookvineng.com

Cover Design by Vine Media
Cover Image from Shutterstock.com

To the heavily criticised NYSC Scheme during which I was inspired
to write most of these stories.

Contents

Kweku's Return

IT WAS THE LOUD CROW of one of Mr. Owusu's chickens that woke Kweku up that morning. He looked out of the diminutive window from his small room. He could see the dew on the grass and the tree branches outside. It was the day he had been eagerly awaiting; the day when the Black Stars will take on their arch-rivals, the Super Eagles, at the on-going African Cup of Nations; the day when Mr. Mensah, the FIFA agent was coming to the Football Academy to scout for players who will go for trials with

European clubs.

Kweku had always dreamt of playing for Liverpool Football Club. He had been a Liverpool supporter since he turned fifteen, three years ago. He had always wanted to be like Michael Essien, to leave the shores of Ghana one day and become a top player in England.

He wanted the fame. He wanted to be able to express himself on a bigger stage than the sandy field of the academy, the inter-academy competitions and the amateur division.

He wanted the money. Each time he looked at the structure he had called home since he could speak, he renewed his resolve to one day be able to move his family to a more decent part of town, away from this slum; and his football talent was the ticket.

He got up from the bed. The sun was out and this meant that he was already late for the early morning jogging session. He began to hurry. His heart began to beat faster. He wouldn't bother brushing his teeth today, let alone taking a bath. He quickly reached for his boots hanging on the wall against the large poster of Michael Essien sporting a Chelsea away jersey.

He reached for his training vest and put it close to his nose. It stunk. He did not remember to wash it before going to bed. He placed it over his shoulder and made for the door.

Outside the house, his mother was cooking in the

kitchen guarded with planks of old wood. He had always admired her hard work and courage. She had been the breadwinner of the family since the death of their father. Neither him, nor his elder sister, Sarah, had the privilege of really knowing who he was as he died months before Kweku was born, when Sarah was barely two years old. But he could almost describe him from the words of his mother and the one picture of him that hung on the wall ever since.

"Good morning mama!" He bellowed to her in the distance.

"Kweku! Come and put something in your stomach before you go."

"*Sorry mama, time don go. I don late.*"

She tried to convince him to wait a little to eat of the beans she was preparing, but he soon took off and screamed something about coming back to eat it in the afternoon as he ran into the cold morning.

*****

The other boys had done a couple of laps around the field when Kweku arrived at the academy, some significant distance from home.

"Give me ten push-ups there!" Coach Bili ordered as he saw Kweku arriving.

Kweku quickly prostrated; his hands and legs to the ground.

"One! Two! Three…" he shouted, pushing up and down until slowly he counted, "Eight…Nine…Ten."

"Good. Join the others!" Coach Bili was in no laughing mood at all. "You know how important today is and yet you chose to come late," he added.

"Sorry sir, I…"

"Shut up and join them!"

"Yes Sir!"

Kweku ran to join the group making their way round the pitch. A few of the boys giggled. They all knew he was the best player in the academy, though they never admitted it. Not a few of them would give anything for him to miss a training session, especially today. He didn't speak to anyone, not even his friend, Johnson.

After three more laps, the coach called the others to sit in the middle of the pitch while Kweku had to do two more. They all sat, panting while the coach stood, staring into the distance with his hands to his back. He seemed just as nervous as the boys themselves. His edginess was more for the fee that would come to him for the sale of a player from his academy than for the players themselves. Kweku was his best bet. But there were a couple of other players who had shown flashes of brilliance over time.

He had seen how Coach Desmond was able to transform the living standard of his family and that of his academy from the sale of two boys to some agents from Paris. He wanted that. He wasn't happy that his academy was not being respected as he thought it ought to be. After all, it was the oldest in the country. But these days, the world seemed to be more interested in how much you make and how many players you have helped to go abroad, and not whether or not you are producing talents that can one day play for the Black Stars – the idyllic aim of academies.

When Kweku joined them, Coach Bili began to talk about how important it was for them to be at their best today. Mr. Mensah was a well respected agent and he had been responsible for several players who have gone on to make it big in Europe. He currently managed top players in the German Bundesliga and the English Premier League. The focus of the training would be more on fitness and skill than anything else.

"Afterwards, we will play a practice match for him to watch and decide based on your performance." He continued, "It is not about whether you have been good before now, if you don't do well today, it means you have lost your chance." He asked them to rest for sometime before proceeding on the regular training for the day. Mr. Mensah should arrive at about mid-day. He walked off into his office to get some rest too.

Kweku finally spoke to Johnson. It was Johnson who spoke first. He asked Kweku why he came late.

"*E be like say I oversleep today, I no even know wetin happen,*" Kweku tried to explain.

"*Na wa o. How today go be now?*"

"How?"

"As in, *how e go be? You dey ready?*"

Kweku wasn't sure how to respond, but he knew he needed to. He also knew that being the supposed best player in the academy, he had to be really careful about his utterances, especially today. He didn't want to sound too confident yet he wanted to hide the fear that had crept up on him since Coach Bili began to talk to them some minutes ago.

"*We go just play our game*. We don't even know how many players the man is looking for," he said finally.

"I heard he wants a striker and a defender. I pray it will be me and you," Johnson smiled and then killed an insect with his boots.

Kweku began to talk about the dream he had two nights ago, about how he arrived in England and completed a successful trial with Liverpool FC and was drafted into the youth team. The others were also in some form of chit-chat about their prospects; a few of them lay on the field trying to get some rest.

Johnson looked on with a broad smile as Kweku talked about the type of house he would move his mother and sister to in one of the estates in town, the type of car he would buy after he completed his trials and began to earn his pounds. Johnson talked about his plan to buy over the land his father sold to send his brothers to school. His heart ached each time he walked past the land and saw his "wicked" uncle farming on the land.

When the training finally commenced an hour later, everyone gave more than a hundred percent. Their dreams were at stake. Today was the reason they all registered at the academy several months ago and for others like Kweku, years ago. They passed, jabbed, controlled and tapped the ball to Coach Bili's amazement. His assistant was also having the same experience with the three goalkeepers at one end of the field. They jumped with more gusto and made incredible saves.

It was now an hour past noon, and Coach Bili kept talking over the phone, trying to find out where Mr. Mensah was and when he would be arriving. Or so the boys assumed. They had gone into another rest session to prepare for the practice match. They had formed two teams and were handed two sets of blue and red jerseys. Kweku and Johnson had been put in different teams which meant he would be playing against Johnson who was a defender.

After another hour, Coach Bili blew the whistle that meant that the boys could come onto the pitch to begin the match, but his countenance betrayed him. He seemed to know something they didn't know.

The boys tried to play their hearts out, but they could not concentrate fully. They kept looking towards the entrance of the academy to see if any one was coming. They could not get their minds off the thought of Mr. Mensah's arrival.

Coach Bili kept screaming intermittently, "Play your game! Concentrate!" as he ran around the pitch, blowing the whistle from time to time for infringments and spot kicks. By half time, he seemed to have found the perfect way to get them to concentrate.

"Mr. Mensah says he will be late and has asked that only the winning team should wait for him." He lied. He saw the faces of the players light up at the sound of that as they reached for satchets of water in readiness for the next forty-five minutes. The next half was completely different from the first. The boys played as though their lives depended on it. It ended goalless and Mr Mensah still didn't come.

*****

His mother could see the fury in his face when he got home. She was sitting outside the frail house, picking seeds of beans to cook. He asked why she was the one doing the cooking and if Sarah wasn't back from school. She told him that Sarah had informed her she would be late from school because of some extra classes she would be attending towards the forthcoming school certificate examinations. Kweku wanted to believe the excuse, but he didn't. He knew Sarah's lateness must have something to do with the new teacher she had a crush on. He wasn't exactly sure who he was or how his sister could like him so soon, but he had overheard Sarah and her friend talk about this new teacher and how all the girls wanted his attention. He hoped he wasn't right. He wanted her to concentrate on her studies like he was concentrating on his football. Her being in school meant he wouldn't get the chance to go to school so he decided to focus on the game he loved.

"*How practise today?*" his mother asked, interrupting his thoughts.

"Fine, mama," his voice quaked. He was glad he wouldn't need to explain whether or not he was picked, or why Mr. Mensah didn't show up. It was wise of him not to have told Sarah and his mother anything was happening today. He had hoped it would be a surprise, to come home and declare that their lives were about to change for good.

"Your food is in the kitchen," she said.

"Thank you mama." He was very hungry. He quickly dropped his boots and training vest; the latter fell on the former on the narrow pavement near his mother. He walked quickly towards the kitchen.

When he came back a few minutes later with the plate of beans, he looked surprised. "*Mama, na beans you wan cook again?*" he queried.

"That's what we have left. Tomorrow, I will go to the market."

He didn't respond as he sat beside her to eat. He should have known that. After the plate was clean, he stood up, *"I dey go watch ball."*

*****

Johnson soon got over the disappointment of not being picked. But it was as difficult as getting the thumb out of the mouth of a sucking child permanently. He didn't eat the first day, but he didn't cry. It wouldn't take him to Paris.

Maybe if it was Mr. Mensah himself that showed up at the academy the day after they expected him, things could have been different, he thought. He would certainly have noticed what an exceptional defender he was and he – Johnson - would be the one on the flight to Paris in a few days. The stout looking, heavily bearded, pot bellied man that came for the selection certainly did not look like a scout to Johnson or any of the boys at the academy for that matter, let alone a FIFA licensed agent. He didn't even sound like one when he said, "You are about to play the match of your lives, because after this game, one of you will be going with me to Paris to play for Paris Saint German." He said Mr. Mensah had sent him since he still wasn't sure if he would be able to make it to the academy due to his "rigid itinerary." Johnson didn't understand that.

But deep down in his heart he was happy for Kweku. He knew that if it boiled down to only one player in the academy, like it did, it had to be Kweku. His goal scoring instinct was top-draw, his speed and agility belonged to men twice his age. His performance on that occasion, he agreed, was exceptional.

*****

The crowd that gathered the evening Kweku left could pass for the entire community, except for a few of the men who had gone for the community elders' meeting. His sister Sarah had helped him pack the few pieces of clothing he had, his boots and jerseys. She too was almost as excited as Kweku himself. She had told almost everyone in school that her own younger brother - "the new Michael Essien" - was going to Paris. She told the new teacher first. She knew he faked his excitement, but she didn't mind.

"Remember the son of whom you are, please." It was Madam Eunice from the next street. "Don't forget our community when you make money, please." She ended most of her sentences with 'please'.

Everyone hugged, pecked and wished Kweku their goodbyes. He didn't even know when the first tear drop strolled down his left cheek. He felt the weight of expectation; the hopes of an entire community.

*****

Johnson still went to the academy, and after each day at the academy, he still had to go sell fruits for his mother at the major road leading to the city. The only thing that changed was that he now wanted to apply for the evening job at the post office to be able to complete his education.

Six months passed and no one heard from Kweku. Except the letter he reportedly sent to his mother after three months about everything being alright very soon. He had asked her to find out the cost of a new house in a better part of the city and was preparing to send Sarah to a better school in the city.

The next time he wrote, he had bought a big house, a big car and was about to come home to pick a wife. He sent them money through the International Money Transfer and asked Sarah to collect it for their mother. He asked them to move out of their house and get a better house in town and transfer Sarah to a better school. He told them that he no longer played football. He was into business.

*****

The few people that gathered the day Kweku's body arrived were those who could find their way to Kweku's mother's new house. The splendor of their new environment left no trace of their former life in the imaginations of people. Sarah, clothed in black apparel, attended to the women sitting in the living room. Some men sat in the compound, under the palm tree, waiting for the others who had gone with Johnson to the airport.

Johnson drove the corpse from the airport in his

new car. He had also brought twelve chickens from his poultry farm, the one he built on the land he bought back after his uncle's death. He was in the company of three men from the elder's council. He had volunteered to take the corpse to the house but when he could not control the tears that flowed freely from his eyes, one of the men was asked to drive the car, the one who tied his wrapper from his chest.

At Kweku's mother's house, some of the women gossiped quietly about the cause of Kweku's death. The woman who sold jewelries to Kweku's mother said he had taken hard drugs in order to be selected by the "white people" from a big football club and the drugs killed him. Another woman from the city said her relative who works at the French Council told her that Kweku swallowed hard drugs to take to some white men in another city in exchange for plenty dollars before the drugs exploded in his stomach and killed him.

Kweku's mother was not allowed to come out from her room. She was not supposed to see her son's corpse or witness his burial. She had asked the women to excuse her from her room; she wanted to be alone to carry out the cruel intentions of her heart to herself.

'SEUN SALAMI

Licentious Romance

IT WAS 10:45PM. Toju was returning from a hassled day at work. It was beginning to rain and he was excited about the fact that he had resumed work barely one month after returning from Nassarawa State. He was grateful to God for that and was determined to prove that he was qualified for the post of Executive Assistant to the CEO which he currently held at Frontline Consulting.

He had just driven past the gas station where he had refilled the petrol tank of his Kia Rio, when he spotted a robust looking lady drenched in the rain by the side of the road. She was alone and looking in different directions rapidly. He thought about helping her.

"Hello! Where are you going?" he yelled after pulling over and rolling down the glass on the passenger's side of his car. The rain was getting into the car.

"Festac," the lady responded, with a relief laden voice. She wiped her face with her hand.

"Please come in."

After she got into the car, her wet dress soaking into the chair, he asked her for her name and what she was doing standing in the rain alone at that time of the night.

"My name is Boma. Thanks a lot for picking me up." She went on about how she had been at that spot for over an hour, even before the rain began, trying to get a taxi going to Festac town. The taxis she saw either wouldn't stop at all or were too expensive for her.

"Where do you work, or are you a student?" Toju asked.

"Yes and No."

"How do you mean?" Toju looked puzzled.

"Please can you turn off the AC, please?"

"Oh, pardon me." Toju turned off the air-conditioner.

"Thanks." She dabbed her arm with a piece of cloth from her bag. "Actually, I am a part-time student of Lagos State University but I also work as a Secretary at an engineering firm."

"Oh, okay - I see." He slowed down for a strider to cross the road and then noticed that her phone kept ringing and each time she would turn off the sound and leave it to ring on. Finally, he decided to ask, though deep down he was sure he didn't need to.

"It is one of these *free* people always disturbing somebody *jare*," she said just before he could ask.

By this time, they were approaching Festac town, so he asked for her address as he maneuvered to turn into the estate.

"I'm really grateful for the ride. I could have been there all night if you didn't show up," she said as he pulled over in front of the house she pointed to on Road 23.

She held on to the handle of the door as if to open it, but then turned to him.

"Do you mind if I have your number, so that if I get stuck again tomorrow, I can call you?" she teased, smiling broadly.

"You're kidding me," Toju said, laughing. "That's okay. Besides, from time to time I hear of job offers here and there, so it wouldn't be a bad idea to keep in touch."

As he stretched out his hand to receive her phone, he noticed her smile again. But it was the first time throughout the ride that he could see her face clearly. She looked more beautiful than he had thought.

"You didn't even tell me where you work and what

you do for a living," she said as he typed his phone number on her phone.

"What's there to say? I am just a young man trying to make ends meet. Nothing special."

"And why aren't you wearing your ring?"

"What ring?" he said, hoping his smile wouldn't give him away.

"Handsome guy, clean car, so nice and caring and no ring? I can't be fooled," she taunted, hoping to get him to talk.

To pacify her, he decided to tell her a bit about himself. He told her about his engagement to Yvonne, a white lady who lives in Ireland, since he thought she wanted to know. He told her about how they had met on the internet and how he travelled to see her from Nassarawa during his service year.

It was now five minutes to midnight and they were still talking. They were laughing loudly, oblivious of the silence around them. He told her about his role as Executive Assistant to the CEO and how he got the job. Boma also told him about the person who had been calling her. She said he was supposed to be her boyfriend, but he was too bossy and so she had decided to call it quits.

"But trust guys, they never give up," she added.

"Well, I don't blame him. Who would give up on a beautiful lady like you?" he asked, and then wished he hadn't.

"Thank you," she said running her hand over her nose. "That's a perfect way to start my day."

"Wow!" Toju screamed as he looked at his wrist watch. "I have to be on my way now. I have to leave for work at 6:30am; you know what they say, 'early to bed, early to rise'."

She thanked him again and finally opened the door. She waved as he drove off. Toju smiled and then promised himself that he wouldn't make any attempt to keep in touch with her. He was no longer sure of his ability to manage advances from ladies. It was a weakness he knew he had to deal with consciously; a weakness that had crept up on him when he met Halima, the chubby daughter of his neighbour, Alhaji Issa, during his National Youth Service in the Nassarawa.

He appreciated her friendship, but Halima wanted much more. After months of consistently throwing herself at him, he finally gave in and started seeing her secretly. The first time it happened was on a Thursday afternoon. He was to go for his Community Development Service, but he felt loath and decided to stay at home. Everyone else in the compound was out except Halima who had just completed her own Youth Service year but was still seeking employment. One thing led to another, and soon, they were on top of each other. He felt as though he was hurting her as she screamed mildly, but all he could think of at that moment was the pleasure between his legs. He felt guilty afterwards and swore never to go close to her again but instead, it soon became a weekly affair and before long, they could no longer control their desire for each other everytime they got the chance to be alone. Since then, he no longer boasted about being able to handle advances from women, it was better to keep a safe distance.

…

Days passed and Toju did not hear from Boma after the text message he got when he got home the day they met – *"Thanks for the ride, it was nice meeting u n talkin wiv u. Rembr me in ur kingdom o…lol. Boma."* He did not reply, so he was surprised when on a Friday afternoon, the following week, he got a text message from Boma requesting to see him urgently after work. He called her immediately to ask if all was well and confirm a venue and time for the meeting. She said she needed to share some things with him and needed his advice on how best to go about them. That day, he didn't wait till 9:00pm as he usually would, to leave the office. By 6:00pm he was off. He told his boss that he would be attending a vigil in church and so needed some time to rest and prepare for it but Mr. Henry Thompson couldn't hide his surprise. He decided to let him go since there really wasn't much for him to do after office hours that day. "Pray for us all and our sinful ways," he had told Toju wittingly.

Toju arrived the *African Kitchen* before Boma. He was just about to start eating the pounded yam and egusi soup which he hoped would be his dinner when he spotted Boma walking into the restaurant. She looked even more beautiful, wearing a tight fitting red top and a pair of blue jeans. He couldn't make out the words on the shirt but he noticed her rounded breasts and hips as she came closer to him. He remembered Halima.

"Hi…hope I didn't keep you waiting for too long?" she asked politely as she pulled out a chair.

"Hope the rain didn't get you today?" he asked smiling mischievously.

"Ha, that is such an unfair thing to say."

They both chuckled. He asked what she would like to eat but she declined.

"I prefer we talk first."

"Hmm…this talk must be very important," Toju responded, before drinking some water. "I'm listening."

"I don't even know if I should be bothering you with my problems," she said, feigning refrain.

"Oh no, come on, that's why I came." He wiped his mouth.

She told him that the house she was living in actually belonged to her friend Kemi, who unfortunately had travelled to see her fiancé.

"So, what exactly is the problem, are you afraid of staying alone?" Toju looked bemused.

"Okay, like…the problem is that I didn't take my own key when I was leaving the house this morning and Kemi wouldn't be back until Sunday to prepare for work on Monday and that means that I…"

"You don't have anywhere to stay, right?" he cut in.

"Yeah."

"So, is that the big issue?" he asked again.

"Can I…"

"Can you stay with me? Why not?"

"Seriously?"

"Yeah, of course you can stay with me." Toju thought he could have offered to pay for hotel accomodation for her but he did not want to seem unkind. Besides, he could do with some extra cash for the weekend.

She got up excitedly and hugged him. "Thanks a lot."

"You're welcome. So, will you eat now?"

"Yeah, why not?" she said, running her hand over her nose.

They both kept mute for a while before Toju said, "we should get you some toiletries on our way home."

…

Toju kept apologising for the state of his house. Boma could sense his discomfort.

"It's okay. Aren't you a guy?" she tried to soothe

him. "I'm sure you would have done all you could to dress it, if you knew someone would be coming home with you. That's how you guys are."

"The thing is, I hardly have time to do anything at home and I don't have anyone here to help with that, you know what I mean."

"No, I don't know what you mean," she smiled as she made for the bedroom with the heap of clothes from the ironing table. "It's a lovely house you've got."

"Thanks." He thought he was being too forward with his teasing. But again he thought that if she was going to be staying with him all weekend, then he had better start talking to her. Afterall, she was making herself at home already.

"I'm sure you can't eat anything again tonight," he said.

"Ah, nothing at all, I'm fine."

"I will still have to find something to chew later. I eat a lot," he presaged.

Two hours later, she was fast asleep in the bedroom, while, he was still typing on his laptop in the living room and monitoring the news on TV at intervals. After the news, he decided to check on her in the room to ensure the air-conditioner was just fine. He had just adjusted the temperature when he heard her soft sleepy voice.

"Aren't you coming to bed?"

He turned to answer her. "I will, but I have to quickly finish the report I am working on."

"*Haba oga*, it's getting late. You have all weekend to do that, don't you?" she queried.

"Don't worry, its just 11:00pm, I'll rest throughout tomorrow."

Soon, her eyes were closed again and not long after he had returned to the living room, he fell asleep on the couch.

…

"So, why did you sleep here last night?" Boma asked as they sat to have dinner the next day.

He responded with an innocent look that suggested he had no excuse. He had expected that she would ask during the day but he had spent most of it sleeping while she watched TV.

"Hope you wouldn't sleep off on the couch today again or you'll start making me feel I am being a bother."

"Why would you say that?"

"I'm kidding, but just don't sleep here tonight. It's your house and you deserve to be comfortable."

"Yes ma. Have you heard from your friend?" he tried to change the subject.

"Who? Kemi?" she said, dropping the spoon of rice she had lifted.

He nodded as he tried to chew the piece of beef in

his mouth.

"She called this morning and I told her I was fine. By the way, can I have something to drink after this?"

"Something to drink?" Toju asked with a surprised look and then gestured to the bottles of water and fruit juice on the table.

"No, not that, I mean something strong…like alcohol."

"Ah, sorry, I don't stock those, since I don't drink," he responded softly, trying to hide his surprise.

"Is there anywhere I can get some, if you don't mind? I'm kind of used to taking it after food."

"Sure, if you check the store down the road, you should get something."

Boma returned very late. She had seen an old friend at the supermarket and they had gone drinking together at a bar two streets away. Toju was already asleep on the couch when Boma banged on the front door. He looked up to the wall clock. It was five minutes to midnight.

"Where have you been? You got me worried," he asked frantically as he opened the door.

"I'm sorry, I ran into an old friend," she apologised, hoping her smile would placate him.

"And why didn't you answer the phone when I called?" he enquired further.

"I didn't leave home with my phone. It's in the

room. At least let me in, *haba oga*."

He could perceive the alcohol on her breath as she walked past him into the living room, running her hand over her nose.

"I'm tired *man*, I need to sleep," she said, as she made for the bedroom, staggering slightly.

"Try to brush your teeth and take a shower before you sleep," he said loudly as she entered the room with the door still ajar.

"Or else you will not join me on the bed as usual!" she exclaimed. "I was going to the bathroom anyway!" she yelled.

He could excuse that. After all, she was obviously under the influence. He soon felt uncomfortable on the couch. He wasn't used to sleeping on it all night and he knew he needed rest. He decided to go in and sleep on one side of his bed. He got up to go in, and then he sat down, and then got up again. As he got near the bedroom door, he could hear Boma snoring loudly. For a moment, he thought about either leaving his trousers on before getting into bed or stripping to his boxers. He would certainly feel more comfortable in the latter. As he got into the bed, he noticed that Boma's back was bare. He looked further down her back before pulling the blanket up from half of her buttocks to cover her naked body and then turning quietly to face the other side of the bed.

Suddenly, he felt himself rising in his shorts. Her

snoring had stopped now. He wanted to get up.

"Thank God, no couch today," Boma muttered as she turned to face him. "Why are you turning your back to me, come on, face here," she said, pressing herself to his back.

Toju could still perceive alcohol, but more than that, he could feel himself being aroused. He hadn't felt this way since he returned from Lafia town.

"Wait, let me turn off the lights," he managed to say as he attempted to get up.

"No, please, don't go to the couch, not again!"

"What is it with this couch, I am coming back, just want to turn off the lights." The stench of alcohol was heavier.

"I thought we agreed that you would brush your teeth and take a shower?" he asked as if talking to the mirror in front of him as he sat on his side of the bed.

"I'm sorry, I had my bath, but I couldn't find the toothpaste."

"It's okay," he said, though he didn't mean it. She must have forgotten, because the toothpaste couldn't have been more conspicuous, sitting on the washbasin in the bathroom. He put his head in his two hands.

Just then he heard his phone ringing loudly from the living room. "Who could that be, at this time?" he muttered. He got up to go but Boma held on to his right hand. "I'm coming, it could be important."

"Promise?"

He chuckled and said, "I promise."

She let go of him.

It was Brother Philip from the church prayer unit. "Hello."

"Hello, Brother Toju. How are you sir?"

"Brother Philip, you've never called me this late. Hope no problem?"

"All is well Brother Toju. I just want to encourage you to be careful, because the devil is after your joy. I saw a revelation as I was praying tonight."

"Thanks sir. I am very fine. I'll be careful." Toju didn't wait to say goodnight before disengaging the phone. Brother Philip was fond of seeing visions. He was just too prayerful, Toju thought. He switched off the phone and went back into the bedroom. He sat back on the bed after turning off the light.

Boma got up from her sleeping position and placed a kiss on his neck with her hands firmly on his chest. "Who was it?"

"A friend," Toju mumbled.

She pulled him closer, planted another kiss on his forehead and then on his lips. He could still perceive alcohol on her breath, but he didn't mind any more. He simply could not resist her now. He thought of pushing her away gently and thinking up an excuse, just then he felt her hands in his shorts. He reclined on the bed…

When he got up to go to the bathroom minutes later, he felt a surge of guilt run through him. He knew the feeling.

...

Toju and Boma got closer with every passing day. So, it was a confused Toju, pacing his office, reading one of a series of text messages warning him to stay clear of Boma or pay with his life. Boma had become his source of happiness in the last few months. Months during which he no longer ate out because Boma was always on hand to do the cooking; months during which he no longer stayed out with his friends, because he knew Boma would be waiting for him at home; months during which he had built his life around her. She had practically moved into his house even though he had never been to her house again since it belonged to Kemi. How could he possibly do without her now? He thought. He informed her about the threats but she denied having any link with it or knowing the telephone numbers used to send the messages. It had become extremely difficult for him to concentrate on anything at work. The week before, he had written 'Boma' instead of 'both' in a report he submitted to his boss. She was all he thought about these days.

He decided that he would close from work early to meet her at her house, before she got ready to come to his, and possibly have a frank talk with her to find out the truth, if there was anything like that. He dialed her phone several times to inform her that he was coming and that she should try to be home early, but he didn't get a response. He decided to go and wait for her.

When he got to her house, the house on Road 23 where he had dropped her off on that rainy night, he could hear loud music from the apartment. He knocked.

"Are you here for the party?" The skinny guy that finally came through the door asked.

"No. I...I'm looking for a lady…Boma."

"Boma? Fat Boma?"

"Yes. Exactly!" Toju's face widened as he tried to raise his voice above the music.

"Boma doesn't live here; she just comes here once in a while."

Toju enquired further and discovered that the house actually belonged to this fellow, whose name he couldn't find the courage to request for. He claimed to have been Boma's boyfriend until two weeks ago.

"Any problem because you are actually asking a lot of questions. I need to get back inside."

"No. No problems at all. Not at all," Toju thanked him for his patience and headed for his car.

He couldn't help thinking about the situation while driving home that night. He had been through so much emotional trauma in such a short time. Now, with the benefit of hindsight, perhaps he shouldn't have responded to the thought of stopping to pick up Boma that fateful rainy day. Or at least, he should have given things a little more time. But then his relationship with Boma had also brought him so much joy, until he began to receive the text messages. He was deep in thought and did not see the oncoming tanker that was trying to use his lane to overtake a saloon car.

"Gboom!"

At the hospital, the doctor said he had lost so much blood and he required an urgent blood transfusion. The elderly man who brought him to the hospital in his Volkswagen Passat had called Boma because her caller name 'My Baby' was the last he had seen on Toju's phone.

"We are of the same blood group so I am sure he can use my blood," Boma said anxiously when she arrived at the hospital.

"Oh, great!" The doctor jumped to his feet. "Please come with me immediately, we need to prepare you for the transfusion."

"Doctor, please nothing must happen to Toju, he's all I've got."

Minutes later, the doctor called her into his office. He was staring at a paper on his table when she entered.

"Doctor, what is wrong? When are we carrying out

the transfusion?"

"I am sorry my dear, we cannot transfuse your blood to him," he was looking straight at her. "Please have a seat. Who did you say you are to him again?"

"His girlfriend…I am his girl…friend," she stammered.

The doctor gave a heavy sigh. "We may need to run tests on Toju as well then," he said under his breath.

"What is it Doctor?" she was raising her voice.

"I am sorry, young lady, but it's not the end of the world."

"What…?" she faded and fell from the chair.

The Doctor jumped up. "Nurse! Nurse!"

Pastor Jay is dead

I HAVE KNOWN PASTOR JOSHUA since we first got into school. When he wasn't a Pastor. He was just like every one of us, trying to get acquainted with registration and school processes. The only difference must have been that he was more pious than the rest of us. It showed.

He was admitted for a Part-time programme, which meant that he would spend five years in the university while we would spend four. But he was in school more often than the rest of us.

The first day I picked him up at the school gate on my way into school, I was driving my dad's Toyota Camry. He introduced himself as if I didn't already know him and then began to preach to me. About giving my life "totally" to Christ and not joining the "*aristo* girls who date married men."

"You can't call yourself a Christian just because you go to church?" I remember him saying.

That was after I told him I was a Christian. I couldn't tell him that I no longer even went to church regularly since I gained admission. I didn't bother to argue further because I could as well listen to the sermon, after all, he was obviously more devout.

You could never find Pastor Joshua in the midst of girls, except those he was preaching to, in the open. His grades after our first year were exceptional and he was well on his way to a First Class. So, I was a bit concerned when he came to invite me for fellowship one afternoon.

"Sister Ropo, I'm inviting you for fellowship this afternoon," he said with a smile, handing me a leaflet. I didn't look at it. I looked up at him.

"Fellowship? In this department?" I was surprised.

"Yes," he beamed. "We are just starting it. In fact, today is our first service," he said excitedly.

"Oh, that's nice," I said and then focused on the leaflet. But deep down I was concerned about him; that he would become more focused on the fellowship activities and begin to lose his good grades. I had heard so many stories about brilliant students who lose everything to religious activities on campus. That was when I began to avoid him. I was neither interested in the fellowship nor "in a closer walk with God" as the leaflet read. It would mean giving up several pleasures in my life. I wasn't ready for that.

***

One session later, the fellowship had grown into something of a phenomenon that everyone was talking about on campus. So I decided to attend one of the services at their new location to see things for myself. I hurried back from the park where I had gone to buy a bus ticket. I was to leave for my fiance's house first thing the next morning.

"Praise the Lord!" Pastor Jay shouted from the pulpit just as I took my seat.

"Halleluyah!" echoed the students crammed in the Chapel auditorium.

Probably encouraged by their response, he shouted again, "I said, Praaaaaise the Looorrrd!"

"Haaaaalleluyaaah!" the congregation echoed excitedly again.

"If you know this is your semester of Discovery for Recovery, and there shall be no carry-over for you, I need you to shout a mighty ha-lle-lu-ya!"

"Haaaaalleluyaaah!" they shouted louder now.

"Tell your neighbour, this is my semester of Discovery for Recovery!"

The congregation obeyed, each one facing the next person and repeating the words, "This is my semester of Discovery for Recovery." I didn't respond to my neighbour. I didn't like his body odour.

"I don't think you understand what I am talking about," Pastor Jay walked down from the pulpit. "I have come to let you know, that this is that semester where everything you have ever lost, will be restored to you in a million fold."

"Ameeeeeeen!"

"Am sorry, but that amen's gat epilepsy! I said this semester, is that semester where all the years the locusts have eaten up will be restored to you in a million fold!"

"Ameeeeeeeeeeeeeen!"

"Greet two people, slap them a high five and tell them, 'This is my semester' and then you may take your seat in the presence of God."

The congregation finally settled down after the greetings and high fives and Pastor Joshua began a message about the importance of Discovery to the pursuit of Recovery. He told the congregation the story of David in first Samuel chapter thirty, verse eight. I had never seen him like this before.

"Please note that the bible specifically tells us that

David inquired at the Lord - shall I pursue this troop? Shall I overtake them? The problem with many of us is that we like to just go, without inquiring of the Lord. If David did not first discover from God, he would not have recovered all."

Almost everyone nodded in agreement each time. A few daring students shouted, "Preach it sir!" occasionally, interrupting the silence that followed every sentence. Pastor Jay moved into the congregation as he explained that the word from God was what made David victorious each time. He diverted to first Samuel chapter seventeen, verse thirty seven. The congregation opened their bibles rapidly. I noticed a sister on the front row whose eyes were fixed on him, she had a red scarf on. He explained that the reason David was able to conquer Goliath was because of the word he had.

"David said you come against me with swords and spares, but I come against you in the name of the Lord God of hosts." He pulled out his hankie from his pocket and wiped his forehead, sweat dripping from his face. "Don't do it if you aint gat the word for it." I felt he was talking to me, and then I wondered about the accent.

About forty minutes had passed and he was now concluding his message. He made a call for a few courageous students who will believe God for a 'Mega Recovery' by sowing a seed towards replacing the fellowship drumset. After three persuasive sentences, ten students walked slowly to the front. I recognized three of them – Sister Tomi,

Brother Tom and Brother Bernard. I joined them.

"As you come forward, begin to challenge God with your seed! Go ahead!"

After the service, Pastor Joshua sat in a corner of the hall, attending to students who needed counsel. The 'excos' were praying in the adjoining corner, I could hear somebody say, "Let's thank the lord for another powerful service." I decided to go and talk to Pastor Joshua about my trip because I was already feeling funny about it after his message.

From the look on each one's face, he seemed to be able to tell what the issue was.

"Pastor Jay, I'm having a test today and I haven't read much. Please I need you to pray with me." It was the lady with the red scarf I had noticed on the front pew.

He held her hands and then asked, "Have you read for the test?"

"Ehn…yes. But not too much."

"Lord, I ask for wisdom for your daughter, that you bless her with insight and foresight and you bring to her remembrance all that she has read, so she can have cause to glorify you."

It was my turn.

The 'excos' had finished praying now.

The lady after me came with a questionable intention. He knew. I also knew as I watched in the distance.

She waited for him to attend to everyone else before her.

"Pastor Jay, your message today was wonderful. You were looking extremely handsome on that pulpit. I just bless God for your life. The woman that will marry you must be very lucky…"

"Thank you, we thank God. Sorry to cut in, how exactly can I help you?"

"Nothing really, I just wanted to tell you how…"

"God bless you sister, please you have to excuse me now, thank you." He stood up from his seat and went to join the 'excos'. I couldn't help the smile that decorated my face.

***

Pastor Joshua was standing at my street junction when I picked him up that morning.

"Pastor Jay! What are you doing on my street today? Evangelism?"

He smiled and said nothing. He looked gloomy. I didn't say anything else.

He handed me a tract few minutes later and said, "Sister Ropo, you need to get closer to God, you may not have a second chance." He still looked gloomy. I simply nodded but didn't say anything.

He asked to alight at the next junction. I asked if he was going to school and he said, "No." He repeated those words about getting closer to God again. I thanked him and drove off.

I usually don't pick calls while driving, but it was Peju who called as I got closer to school. She probably wanted me to come pick her up, but I was already almost in school and I needed to let her know that.

"Hi Peju, me I'm almost in school *oh*, you have to find your way."

"You can't even greet. I'm already in school."

"Oh oh. So, what's up?"

"Have you heard?" she said as if she didn't want anyone around her to hear her.

"Heard what?"

"Pastor Jay is dead."

I felt I didn't hear her clearly, so I asked, "Which Pastor Jay?"

"How many Pastor Jays do you know? Pastor Joshua, the departmental fellowship pastor of course." I didn't talk. She continued, "I don't have much credit, I just heard that they had an accident two days ago on their way back from their National Convention and he was the only one that died. His obituary is all over…" The phone went off.

I was speechless. I thought about the fact that Peju must have been flippant, but then I remembered that she wasn't given to pranks, especially those about death. I took a very deep breath and heaved a very heavy sigh. I wanted to park the car but I decided to get to school first.

As I drove through the school gate, I saw a black and white poster with Pastor Jay's picture. There was no 'Obituary' on it, but it had the words PASTOR JOSHUA IS DEAD. That was when I began to cry. I was in shock, at the death but I was confused because I had picked Pastor Jay up and dropped him off on my way to school. I walked towards the poster to look closely. Under the large print were details of his department, year of birth and death, seperated by a dash. It also had the information Peju had given me, about an accident while returning from a Convention. I walked back to the car.

***

The following week at the cemetery, I was speechless all through the ceremony, just as I had been all week and at the church service earlier in the day. I had not told anyone about the experience that morning on my way to school. I would never tell anyone. Who would believe such anyway?

I remembered how Pastor Jay saved me from imminent death, that day after the fellowship when he warned me not to travel the next day. He said he could sense danger. I obeyed him and told my fiance that I wouldn't be able to come. That began the process that eventually led to our break-up, but I was more than content. I would later hear that the bus I was to board to Port-Harcourt that morning was involved in an accident. Only one person died; the woman that took my seat, seat number 2. "So, why couldn't Pastor Jay sense danger this time?" I wondered to myself.

As his casket was lowered into the grave amidst wailing and howling, the vanity of life suddenly hit me. "Is this how it will all end?" I asked myself.

Right there, I made a decision. I said a simple prayer to God and asked him to forgive my sins. I promised Him that if it took the death of Pastor Joshua to get me closer to him, I was ready to live for him from then on.

The Son of your Father's Concubine

MY JAWS DROPPED FIRST. Then my bag. Then my phone. I picked them up and made for the exit.

"Sister! Sister! What is the matter?" He didn't recognise me.

I was pleased. No I wasn't. I wanted to scream. I wanted to strangle him. I wanted vengeance. But more than that, I wanted to wake up to discover that it had all been a dream. All – the last one year of my life, especially that Saturday morning; that Saturday of Easter.

***

"Spread your legs! Spread it! Or you want me to *chuke* you?"

***

I had been best friends with God since my first year in the university. Best friends. I was the sort of girl you would call a church girl. I practically lived there. I was a member of the choir, the prayer unit and also the Vice-president of the youth fellowship. I was also the most sought-after spinster. Until that morning.

That night was the special Good Friday combined zonal praise night. It was the night I led the choir in that glorious rendition of the Halleluyah chorus. It brought the heavens down, literally. It was the night I received the most compliments for a single ministration with the choir. Unknown to me, it would herald the day I would also receive the most bruises. Emotional. Physical. Psychological.

The morning of the Saturday of Easter was to be environmental sanitation Saturday, but it was cancelled. It was also the wedding day of my childhood friend, Chinwe. I wanted to get home early enough to get some rest before going to get my first chief bridesmaid experience; but since I had already taken my things to her house, I decided to go there to get some rest before the morning.

It was not the first time I would go through Karounwi Street to Chinwe's house on Thomas Street, but there was something different about this morning. I could feel it in my throat as I walked through the shops in front of the house with the tall fence. Everywhere was quiet. My eyes raced through the beginning of the street to the end, only a couple of goats lay beside their faeces on the road.

I took three more steps and there he was: a huge bare chested masculine frame at the corner to my left. A deliberately broken beer bottle in his left hand, a hurriedly folded wrap of hemp between two fingers in his right hand, emitting smoke and a repulsive odour.

"If you run, you are dead." His voice was husky. I had lost mine. He walked towards me. He grabbed me and pulled me to the open space in front of one of the shops. He ordered me to lie on my back or he would use the bottle on me. I pleaded but he wasn't listening. He looked like one taking instructions from an invisible force. The floor was cold and bare. My bible dropped beside the wrap of hemp and the broken bottle.

***

"Please, I'm a virgin, please don't do this!"
"Shut up! Keep quiet or I will *chuke* you!"
***

I didn't discover the pregnancy until it was three months old. What did I even know about pregnancy or getting rid of it? Who could I tell and how would I explain it? The pain I endured that night was not just between my legs, but between my ears and at the left side of my chest. It has continued until now.

Everyone tried to get me to tell them the father of my unborn child. The pastor. My mother. My father. The head of our family – the short old man who always had kolanut in his mouth or pocket. He suggested that we could arrange a wedding so that the baby could be born, knowing his father. I didn't want that. Not that father.

I had let the church down. 'The holy sister who got pregnant before marriage'. I had been the epitome of chastity, until it was taken from me forcefully by the fear of the piercing of a broken bottle. But my heart was now pierced by the thought, the voice. Still, the father of my unborn child remained in my memory and in their imagination. I made sure.

During those months, I was like a dog smitten with an ailment. Everything got to me. I neither talked nor mingled with anyone except myself. When I managed to eat, I would take a spoon or two and the food would lose savour or was it me who had lost a sense of taste? What fed me were my tears and the pain I was now getting used to.

As the evidence of my 'immorality' protruded beyond the covering of my regular clothes, I stopped going to church. I had to. I had become the laughing stock, or at least the talking point. I who used to sing and the heavens will descend. I was now THE STUBBORN PREGNANT LADY WHO IS PROTECTING THE IDENTITY OF

AN IRRESPONSIBLE LOVER. I wished they were correct.

It was not the life I was used to, but it was one I had to live. I moved out of my parents' home when the shame got too much for them to bear. They risked losing their titles in the cathedral if they kept harbouring a pregnant daughter who was not married. I went to live with my grandmother on the outskirts of town.

Mama was very kind to me. She taught me patiently and prepared me for another type of pain that was to come. One that was like no other that I had experienced before then.

I couldn't tell whether my baby resembled his father because I did not see his face clearly except it came along with that voice. But I was sure my baby did not look like me in any way, except that she cried a lot and Mama would say, "That is how you used to cry too." I made sure I didn't cry when she used the towel dipped in hot water to mop my belly and when she made me sit in warm water.

***

"Very sweet…you are a very, very sweet girl."

***

His voice kept echoing in my head. I spat each time

it did. It was the reason I spent longer washing between my legs than my entire body; that voice. It was the reason I decided never to let a man come close to me again.

The naming ceremony could have passed for a funeral, except that there was no casket and we didn't sing a dirge. Mama was my only comfort. She carried and cuddled Enitan like the human being that she was. My mother also did, but I could see the difference. My father barely sat down all through the ceremony as he kept pulling out the antenna of his cellular phone to receive all manner of calls. Yet, I couldn't be mad at him, afterall he was the one giving Mama money to take care of Enitan and me.

Saturday of Easter was approaching again, and it was now almost a year since I had been to the house of God. For half of that period I had not opened my bible. Prayer was not even in the picture. Not that I was angry with God. It was his people I could not forgive. How come nobody dared to imagine that something could have gone wrong on that Saturday of Easter? Couldn't my parents notice that it was after then I began to seek solitude and shed tears often? How come the brethren simply concluded that I must have been 'fornicating' to be pregnant?

But I knew I wasn't myself. I felt the vacuum like a garage that had been taken over by weed for lack of a car to park in it. I knew I had to mend bridges with my creator. After all, He had still been merciful to me, even though his people weren't. I didn't deliver Enitan in a hospital. It was

Mama who midwifed me, but he was still merciful. How would I begin to mend this long broken bridge?

I remember the night I finally told Mama the whole story, shortly after Enitan was born. She comforted me and assured me that I wasn't the first to experience such at my age. The difference was, in her own case, she didn't get pregnant. I couldn't believe my ears. But I felt lighter. I had finally opened up to someone, the only person who had shown me real love through my ordeal; the only person reputed in our family to be the custodian of all of the family's secrets.

I decided I would return to church, but definitely not Trinity Cathedral. They didn't deserve to have me back. They wouldn't even want me. I would find another church in another part of town. Maybe with time, I would begin to find my place again.

Sunday came and Sunday went, but I kept procrastinating. Sunday after Sunday, week after week, "How would I feel in the midst of people?" I thought often. Even my legs had gotten used to being indoors, all by myself. Once in a while, I would come out to help mama at her small provision shop, but how many people came there in a day?

Then I thought, maybe I should start by facing one person. Maybe a pastor. He would be able to help me get out of my anger and bitterness.

But when he said, "You are welcome sister. God

bless you. Please have a seat." I couldn't gaffe that voice, even in my sleep. That was when my jaws dropped. Then my bag, then my phone.

I picked them up and made for the exit.

"Sister! Sister! What is the matter?" He didn't recognise me.

When I got home and told Mama what had happened, she sang several proverbial songs and danced to them in circles for several minutes. She picked up Enitan, danced around with her singing something in my language about her head being correct and not being without covering.

I couldn't fathom her joy. She didn't seem to see things my way. The man who had caused this much pain in my life was the same man I had gone to, to help restore my relationship with God, and Mama was dancing?

But she wasn't dancing about that. She always seemed to see everything through a positive lens. My explanation hadn't even occurred to her. She was dancing because, "God works in mysterious ways." She was dancing because *"Ibi aye foju si, ona o gba be."* Something in my language that sounds like, 'Man proposes but God disposes'. She was dancing because God had finally vindicated me. Her too, for standing by me through it all.

I still harboured vengeance, and not even Mama's joy could wipe that away. How could he just go scot free after what he did to me? I was sure I wouldn't have been the only one he would have raped. God had to be just. How could he have become a pastor just one year after what he did to me? How? God had to explain this himself. Was He so easy to pacify?

***

"You are welcome sister. God bless you. Please have a seat."

***

The nights that followed were rather bizarre. I heard that voice more frequently. After I did, Enitan would begin to cry. She would cry so hard that I would be confused. Mama told me to pull up my blouse for her each time, and then she would feast till she slept. It continued for one week.

"This child is telling us something," Mama had begun again with her superstition. "These old people *sef*," I thought. What if I told her I still heard that voice often, and that as soon as it stopped was when Enitan would begin to cry? Maybe then, she would find a connection. I was beginning to find one myself already.

The next day was when my parents visited. They wanted me to return home but Mama would have none of that. "Did she tell you I am suffering her here?" she asked, hissing consistently.

"Mama, it is not like that, but she has to return home and continue with her life." My mother was untying the tubers of yam they brought for Mama. "Maybe she can find a man that will marry her," she said in a lower pitch.

I coughed. It wasn't involuntary. I couldn't imagine that. Somehow I hoped Mama wouldn't tell my mother about the pastor. I hoped it would remain a secret between us – Mama and me.

***

Mama agreed to go with me to the church during the Easter celebration. We would not go on Sunday. Mama said she didn't want to attend a service where she would have to give an offering that she wasn't sure where it would end up. She had always thought like that. We would go to the pastor's office on Saturday. Saturday of Easter. I had seen that he usually attended to visitors for counseling on Saturdays from noon. I am not sure why I wanted Mama to come with me, but I guess it was the feeling of knowing an elder would know how things like this should be handled.

It didn't look like a church service when we got to the church but there was a crowd in the church premises, shouting and wailing. Many of them were in black. I spotted a fair woman whom many other women were holding, consoling. Two young boys that couldn't have been more than four and six years old were standing beside her. There was a coffin.

My legs weakened suddenly. My heart began to beat

faster. My throat dried up quickly. Then I looked closely at the picture placed in front of the coffin. A man, dark with a brief mustache. I wasn't sure.

"Please, who died?" I asked an old woman beside me.

"A-a-are you new here?" she asked amidst what I sensed were crocodile tears, instead of answering my question.

I quickly turned to the man next to her. "Please, who died sir?"

"Our son *oh*, our son is dead *oh*! Chei!" he wailed.

Our son. I was getting impatient. Mama had hurried to meet me now.

"Who did they say died?" she asked me in Yoruba.

"I don't know yet mama." I dashed past the crowd and headed for the pastor's office. I still knew where it was. A few women sat on the couch at the reception like vegetables soaked in salt water. Mama was behind me. I could hear her hasty steps and the splatter of her slippers. I didn't knock.

"Excuse me madam, I still have some visitors in here." He got up from his chair. The couple in front of him turned to look at Mama and me as though they had seen the man in the coffin outside. I heaved a very heavy sigh when I heard his voice. It was the first time that voice had brought me relief.

"Please madam, we have a programme going on and

we are still busy. Besides, it's not polite to enter the pastor's office without knocking," the woman said.

I wanted to talk, but Mama did first. "Kamoru!"

The pastor's face roused like a teenage girl who had been stripped naked in public. The couple got up to leave.

"Kamoru, *iwo ni?*" Mama shouted again, this time pointing at the pastor.

"Mama, do you know him?" I managed to say.

"*Ha! Aye o!* Kamoru!" Mama's hands were on her head, removing her head tie.

"Mama *agba*?" the pastor murmured.

I held Mama's hands. My nerves were in shreds. Only those who truly knew Mama ever called her that. "Mama, who is he?"

"*Ha!* Abeke."

"Who is he mama?" I shouted.

She held my hands tightly, took a deep breath and said, "This is your younger brother. The son of your father's concubine."

Greenland Reverie

SEGUN HAD JUST COMPLETED HIS NATIONAL YOUTH SERVICE. The colourful passing-out parade ceremony had just ended and he had led a quarter-guard during the parade. Now he was sitting in the subway train that conveyed the discharged corps members from the parade ground to the employment pavilion where officials from various multinationals had set up tents waiting for the discharged corps members.

"Have you made up your mind which of the offers

you would opt for?" he turned to ask Ngozi. She shook her head. He smiled as he said, "Even I don't know yet. I will decide today anyway."

He had received an email from *Gainers Bank* and two other companies confirming his appointment. One of the companies had offered him the post of Media Manager, a job that came with an official car and accommodation. But he preferred to be the Assistant Public Relations Manager at the Bank. He had always admired the Bank and he would earn more there while having access to loans and mortgages.

"I think I'll go for the *Gainers* offer," he said finally.

"So, my husband will be joining those bankers?" Ngozi mused, dropping her head on his shoulder.

He looked away to the other side of the train and saw some of his friends in similar debates over which offer was more lucrative, which one had more financial security and which one guaranteed fulfilment. He spotted Kelvin in his usual full NYSC regalia; his voice was the loudest.

"I will rather go for ConnectFund. This is 2033 my brother. How many banks will be in operation in the next ten years? How many of you will know what cash looks like by that time?"

"*Efribody* cannot be computer and credit card like you." It was Aminu, with his northern accent that always stood him out among their friends.

Segun thought about their discussion briefly, before the sound of the train stopping disrupted his thoughts. They had arrived at the station and his heart was suddenly beating faster. As they came unto the mainland from the tunnel and walked some distance towards the pavilion, he noticed two ladies in suit in front of the pavilion with the familiar 'G' logo of the *Gainers*. He held Ngozi firmly before walking across to them.

"Good Afternoon, I'm for your bank," he said proudly.

"Oh, you are welcome sir," one of the ladies said before leading them to the tent.

The pavilion was getting busier, with several negotiations going on here and there. Ngozi had also left to find the tent of the Nigerian Customs Authority, NCA.

"Did you get an email?" was the first question on the interactive machine with a YES and NO option on the screen. He quickly touched the YES button. He couldn't believe that his hands were beginning to shake. The machine posted a few other questions to which he responded. Minutes later, his eyes were darting around the pavilion with the print-out of his letter of appointment. He was looking for Ngozi, or at least the NCA tent. The pavilion was now very busy. He walked quickly along the footpath to a Customs officer in uniform.

"Please where is the NCA tent?" he asked the smart looking officer. But just before the officer responded, he heard that inimitable voice from behind him.

"Baby! I've been looking all over for you."

He turned, "Hey!" and then turned to thank the officer before holding Ngozi's left hand in his right.

"Let me see that."

He collected her appointment letter in exchange for his before saying, "I knew you would settle for Customs."

She smiled and asked, "What brand of car?"

"I don't know, but I've seen some of their cars, most of them are Nira B5s.

"That's what they are giving me too," Ngozi said.

They laughed. Segun thought briefly about the fact that the NCA didn't have a choice than to use electric cars made in Nigeria, but the cars had to be good for most of the banks and multinationals to also be using them.

"So, where are we going now?" Ngozi asked.

"To celebrate of course!" He planted a kiss proudly on the left side of her mouth before saying, "Now you will have all the authority in the world to fight injustice." Ngozi simply smiled.

At *Food Court* a few buildings away, after placing their orders, he turned as if to be sure Ngozi was still there. She smiled. As they sat down, him carrying the tray with ofada rice and beef, Ngozi with the water bottles, he finally managed to mumble, "I will miss you."

"What do you mean?" Ngozi replied, "We are going to Lagos together incase you don't know. At least you are not resuming until next month."

"I hear!" Segun said with a mocking accent

mimicking the soldiers on the NYSC camp.

This was the moment he had waited for, this 'going to Lagos together'. But now mixed emotions enveloped him. He quietly hoped that, miraculously, his mother would have changed her views about inter-tribal marriages before he got the chance to take Ngozi home. She was a good girl after all and that is what his mum had always asked for.

...

Inside the elevator of the Tejuosho Modern Market, Segun was familiar with the fragrance of the lady in the white blouse and blue skirt. Ngozi's friend, Tonia had introduced *Be Inspired* from House of Tara to them. He had liked it from that first day. He wasn't really sure what it was about the perfume that attracted him; the case shaped like a plaque with the world on top or the whiff itself. For a moment he thought about Tonia.

His mum's boutique was on the fourth floor. He could still remember the joy she felt when the shops were re-allocated after fire razed the original Tejuosho Market several years ago. As he entered the brightly coloured boutique, he could hear his mother's voice at the corner. *Iya Segun* – as her friends called her - always raised her voice when she discussed anything she really cared about. She was in a discussion with her three friends, the only friends she kept, about their next trip to buy goods for their various shops. Mrs. Jibokun was pregnant with her third child, while Romoke, the youngest of the friends was a single parent. Her daughter Bola was studying Aeronautic Engineering at the Ahmadu Bello University. Only Mrs. Wellington still visited Dubai once in a while, especially because of her husband. The others preferred Tinapa.

"You people know I have to go to Dubai," Mrs. Wellington said.

Mrs. Abdul raised her voice again, "*Dubai ko, Dubai ni!* Better tell your husband to quickly finish what he is doing there and come and make some money here."

The friends had a good laugh, but Mrs. Wellington didn't look too happy. For her, Segun could not have come in at a better time.

"*Eku ile ma,*" he greeted in Yoruba, bending slightly as if something hindered him from prostrating fully, something invisible.

"*Ah...oko mi,*" Mrs. Abdul got up to hug her son, a little too tightly.

"*Haba,* don't squeeze the poor boy dry *jare,*" said Romoke. She was holding her phone to her cheek.

When Mrs. Abdul released her grip, Segun explained that he had been to the house to drop his bags. His flight was right on time and everything had gone smoothly.

"So, did you get something to eat?" she asked with an admiring look.

"We ate in the plane," Segun responded.

The *Air Nigeria* flight from Owerri to Lagos was probably the best he had been on in a long time. Ngozi definitely made it all the more interesting. But for him, the economy class didn't feel like 'economy'. The air hostesses were extremely polite, almost to a fault. The seating arrangement and order in the plane, he thought, was exceptional.

"Hope you were easy on those Igbo girls *oh*," Mrs. Wellington was in her impish mood.

"Please *oh*, my son is a pastor." Mrs Abdul was walking away to help her attendant attend to a seemingly difficult customer she had noticed, it was something about the customer's payment card.

"So, when are we meeting the Igbo girl your mother talked about?" Mrs Wellington was not done.

"We came back together but she had to go see her mum too." Segun was relieved they had asked. Something inside him spawned excitement whenever he got the chance to talk about Ngozi.

"She is really looking forward to meeting everybody too." He reached for the copy of *VineStyle* on the table as if to say he wanted to wait till his mother came back to join the discussion. He didn't want to have to repeat himself. He tried to concentrate on the picture of the President on the cover. He had always been awed by the President's dress sense. If he was on a native attire, it would be uniquely designed, and if he was on a pair of suit, the tie would stand out. He had always wondered who was responsible for knotting those trademark ties. He thought briefly about the last speech he heard the President deliver at the presentation of the appropriation bill that was televised on National TV. He remembered how he had concentrated more on the green tie he had on, rather than the eloquent speech. His mother had returned to her seat now. Her friends had continued the conversation.

"And do we have a date yet?" Mrs. Wellington looked away mischievously.

"That reminds me Segun, your father also wants us to speed up the process," Mrs. Abdul said quickly, almost rushing.

"What? You told dad?" Segun looked scared now.

"What do you mean, you told dad?" she mimicked him and then muttered a Yoruba proverb about the father being the one to eventually resolve a previously kept secret.

"Did you tell him she was Igbo?" he asked, still looking scared.

"Of course I did."

"And what did he say?"

"That he trusts your judgement and that he would love to meet her when he comes back next week."

"Hmm…hmm," Mrs. Wellington was faking a cough.

Then Romoke got up. "Maybe we should give mother and child some time to talk. Just make sure you let us know the date on time."

"So we can prepare for *Aso Ebi* on time," Mrs. Wellington added.

"*Aso Ebi ko, Aso Ebi ni.*" Mrs. Abdul joked. She thanked her friends for spending time with her. She walked them to the corridor and turned back at the elevator. Segun had walked across to the attendant and had started a conversation about how the East was very different from Lagos.

"Segun!" Mrs Abdul called out. She didn't look suspicious. He had hoped she wouldn't.

"And what did she have to say?"

"Who?" he asked as if he didn't know.

"Mr. who *ni,*" she said mockingly and continued, "Ekaete of course. Or who were you talking to?"

"Oh, she was just asking how Owerri was and all that."

"The girl is fond of arguing with customers these days." She reached for her slippers under the chair with her legs almost idly and then asked, "So, what exactly is your plan with Ngozi?" looking straight ahead as though she had said nothing.

"Marriage ma." He swallowed his saliva. "We've discussed it and we think we are ready for it."

"Segun, you think, or you are ready?" she was looking serious now.

"We are ready. We know."

"Hmm…*temi ye mi o*. Marriage is more than husband in bank, wife is working with NCA, we have money; let's marry…"

"I understand all of that mum," he interrupted her. "I'm sure about this."

"OK. That was exactly what I told your dad; that for you to have come to this point, you must have really thought about it." She reached for her Fendi eyeglasses on the table. "The earlier we start preparing for the wedding, the better."

…

The wedding took place exactly a month later. It was on a Saturday; at Christ Church, Owerri, where Ngozi's family had been members for thirteen years. The service was extremely brief and they had proceeded to the reception at the five-star Concorde Hotel Plus. Arrangements had been made for them to have their honeymoon at Obudu in Cross River State.

As he sat next to Ngozi in the back seat on the way to the airport, Segun wasn't sure of what to think about first. One thing he was sure about was that he had never felt so much peace. He had Ngozi's left hand in his right, an involuntary habit he had developed. He observed the neatly trimmed lawns that divided the roads and the serenity of the streets. He thought about the flight and the week long experience he would have with Ngozi. He almost couldn't believe they were now married.

"Honey, you look lost," she interrupted his thoughts.

"Do I?" He turned to her and planted a kiss on the side of her head. He could hear the sound of a train approaching on the other side of the road as the driver manouvered towards Airport Road.

"I don't know why, but I think you were thinking about the honeymoon," she followed up.

"Yeah. And then I'm just so glad I married you."

"Me too, dear. So, so glad," she said and then dropped her head on his shoulder.

As the plane set out to take off after the in-flight announcements, Segun couldn't have been more relieved. The attention on them from the departure area to the aircraft had gotten to him. Ngozi had noticed his look and in her usual way pacified him. After all, she thought, they were newly weds and anyone who wanted to admire them was welcome.

For some minutes after take-off, they talked about the wedding ceremony. They had noticed Kelvin, Aminu and Bade at the church, but the trio had left after the ceremony to catch their various flights.

"Remind me to call Kelvin when we land," he said.

"No problem." She had already thought of making an appreciation list that would contain the names of the guests that had honoured them. Then again she thought of teasing Segun for a bit.

"But can't that wait till our honeymoon is over? People are not supposed to hear from us until about a week."

"Hmm, says who?"

"Says the 'Fourteen laws of honeymoon'," she joked.

"And that must be authored by my dear Ngozi Abdul."

"You wouldn't even wait for me to declare my change of name by myself!"

They laughed.

Just then, the in-flight announcer's voice was back. He explained that there were signs that the flight might experience slight turbulence due to unprecedented weather conditions. He however urged passengers to be calm and that all was well.

Ngozi stretched out and held his right hand in her left. Segun could almost feel her pulse racing. He tried to calm her down, explaining that it was one of those things that happened once in a while on flights and that they would get through it.

Minutes later, the plane began to shake like a car going over several road bumps. Ngozi was holding on tighter now. Segun could see another woman on the opposite row clinging to her husband. He could also hear someone say 'Jesus' behind them. Just then, it felt like the plane was going down. The voice of the announcer was back, but this time it was hasty.

"Passengers, please release your life jackets as earlier demonstrated, we are losing altitude."

"Jesus! Jesus!" The voice behind him screamed louder.

"This is not my portion! I reject this. I shall not die but live!" Another woman was shouting repeatedly from the back. The man in front of them had both his hands on his head; he was calling out "*Allahu akbar*" repeatedly. Segun could feel the plane going down faster. He tried to concentrate on the life jacket.

The announcer's voice was back. "We are sorry about the situation. Passengers please put on your life vests and follow the instructions. We have lost 7,000 feets. We need to evacuate the aircraft as quickly as possible. Everything will be fine if you don't panic." His voice was stern.

The panic became even more severe after the announcement. Segun's heart was beating uncontrollably now. He could feel his pants wet with urine. He tried to concentrate on the flight attendant at the entrance of the plane. She too was shaking. He strapped Ngozi with her life jacket first, then his. She was crying. He tried not to.

"Don't worry dear. We'll be fine," he whispered, his voice trembling.

The plane was going down much faster now. Suddenly it skewed towards their side, still going down. The screams became louder. Only a few people didn't have their life jackets on now. Three attendants hurried to help them, holding on to seats to make their way. The announcer's voice was very loud this time.

"Ladies and Gentlemen, we are heading for a crash landing. Please stay calm as we make our way out through the emergency exits. Please follow all instructions, we will all be fine. I wish you the best of luck."

…

Segun woke up at exactly 9am. He was sweating profusely.

It couldn't be true, he thought to himself before jumping out of his mattress that lay on the bare floor. He quickly checked the Covenant University calendar that hung on the same nail he had hung his NYSC cap. It confirmed his fears.

"March 2009?" Then he saw the date he had marked just the night before. The passing-out parade of Batch A Corp members – 'March 26, 2009'. It meant today was March 3. He remembered that he had celebrated when the announcement was made only yesterday, and he had told himself that he had less than 23 days to spend in Imo State.

He looked around his room. It was his room, he knew. The near empty room that he had called home for nearly one year now. He couldn't deny it. The reading lamp on the table, his jungle boots, sandals and shoes just behind the door. At the other end, piles of clothes he would wash on Thursday before going for his Community Development Service. He took two sluggish steps back to his bed and sat helplessly, his head in his hands.

"So it was all a dream. I can't believe this."

He felt the vibration of his phone on the bed before quickly raising his pillow to pick it up.

"Hello dear," he muttered.

"Hey Baby…what's wrong? You sound cold." It was Ngozi.

"I had a dream; it scared the life out of me."

Ngozi tried to calm him down. She asked him to get dressed and meet her in school because she was already on her way.

The walk to the State Secondary school was longer than usual. He thought again about the tarred roads and the buses he had seen in his dream, picking him up every day to his place of primary assignment. He couldn't believe all that he had seen was only a dream. He stopped by to say hello to Ngozi in JSS2 classroom before heading for JSS1 classroom where he was to teach Social Studies at 10am.

He looked at the wall clock, he was ten minutes late.

"Good morning class," he said finally after waiting for the class to settle down in a rush. He picked up a broken piece of chalk from the floor before asking the class, "Did you guys bother to sweep this class this morning?"

The whole class looked surprised. He had never bothered himself about the state of the classroom. All he bothered about in the school was Ngozi and the two subjects he taught – Social Studies and Christian Religious Studies.

"Anyway, today we will be discussing 'The Family.'" He turned to write on the board.

After the class, he walked to Ngozi's classroom, but she was still teaching. She always exceeded her period and whenever he complained, she would say, "Mathematics takes longer to assimilate." He didn't want to go into the class today, so he waited for her to look his way before giving a sign that meant he would be back. He had to be at the NYSC Secretariat to confirm if the persistent error on his name had been finally rectified. A slapdash typist had omitted the 'g' in his name and so his call up letter had read 'Seun Abdul' instead of 'Segun Abdul'.

He wished his dream had not been just a dream, he wished it could be reality, leaving out the plane crash he was about to experience. He wished he didn't have to throw his CV around to several companies after March 26. After all, even if the school would retain him, he wasn't ready to stay in this state. Not with the N3, 000 they managed to pay him every month.

As he alighted from the bus, just in front of the secretariat, he made up his mind that he was going to do everything he could to deliver this future he had seen. He would set up an advocacy group that would spread this message of a new Nigeria to as many as would care to listen.

"Yes? Where do you think you are going dressed like that? Go back!" the security guard at the secretariat shouted.

It took a few seconds before Segun realised that he was not in his NYSC uniform and there was no way he could enter the secretariat that way. His hands dropped to his waist, and then he refused to accept that he should have remembered, after all he was consumed by the desire to get the name error corrected to avoid having 'Seun' on his discharge certificate. His phone beeped. It was Ngozi. He dialed her number twice before it rang.

"I'm leaving the secretariat; I'll join you in school before you know it."

Ngozi was his only consolation for coming to Imo State. She was an indigene and that made things a bit easy for him. She was serving in the state because her uncle, Chief Odoemelam had helped her with the posting arrangement.

"I couldn't watch and allow our *Omalicha* go and suffer in the hands of your people," he had told Segun the day they met, before adding, "and she must not suffer in your own hands, *inugo*?"

He and Ngozi had met at the registration hall of the NYSC Orientation Camp in Umudi. He liked her from the moment she said, "Please don't allow anybody join the line *oh!*" as he tried to sneak into the long queue of people waiting to be registered. After the registration, he walked up to her and asked why she had opposed his joining the queue from the young man in front of her and she answered austerely, "I hate injustice."

They would later become the most famous couple on camp, and unlike the others, they were posted to the same local government, the same school.

"I'm sure you *worked* it," Yewande had accused Ngozi on the day the letters were distributed after the final parade on camp.

"Sincerely, we didn't know anything about it, it just shows how true our love is," Ngozi had responded proudly. It meant that while others were crying and sharing tight hugs, they would continue to see each other everyday.

The overwhelming thought of his dilemma suddenly returned. He loved Ngozi. He had never been more certain about anything. But *Iya Segun* would not hear of such. He had kept his relationship with Ngozi away from his mother because she had reminded him the last time he traveled home not to "make the mistake" of loving an Igbo girl.

"You will find a good wife here when you finish your service," she had said.

But he wanted to be able to take Ngozi home to his parents; he wanted them to support him to raise the huge bride pride he knew her people would demand.

He was now getting closer to the school before his

phone beeped again. Then he thought of bringing up the issue of marriage with Ngozi today, especially his mother's dislike for Igbo girls. The few times they had talked about it, it was Ngozi who instigated it, teasingly telling him to prepare to 'buy' her from her parents, "Of course you already know I am not cheap," she had said with that smile that Segun had come to love.

Quarter Past Midnight

"HELP! PLEASE HELP US!"

Gabriel could hear Emmanuel screaming as he ran into the ground floor of the hospital, carrying him. He could feel the pain running through his spine; he could see the blood on Emmanuel's shirt, his blood.

The nurse at the reception quickly ran into an adjacent room, and then ran out about a minute later with another nurse, carrying a stretcher.

Just then, Gabriel began to feel as though he was

floating. He could feel less of the pain now. As they laid him on the stretcher into the emergency room, he wished for a moment that he could return to a few weeks ago, when he was just a 'mummy's boy'.

He had always been a 'mummy's boy'. It wasn't just his nickname amongst his friends. The first time he was told he would be transferred to Kings' College, he had begged his mother to allow him remain a day student. The thought of going to the boarding house had always frightened him. He had wondered how he would cope, living without his mum and dad. He was the only child of the Enebelis and he had come to depend so much on his mother, Mrs. Enebeli. She was a Doctor at St. Nicholas Hospital. Gabriel could not wait to return home from school everyday just to give his mummy a hug. The first time he told his SS1 classmates that he hugs his mum, they laughed him to scorn and nicknamed him "Mummy's boy." But he didn't mind.

"You'll be fine Gaeb. I'll make sure I check on you every week. The school is not far from the hospital." Mrs. Enebeli herself wasn't entirely convinced about having Gabriel at the boarding house. He was her only friend especially now that his father usually returned late from work. He had just secured a major road construction contract that required a lot of his time.

But Mr. Enebeli would have none of that. "This boy is going to end up spoilt. He needs to see life the way it is. Let him mix with other people's children and learn to fight for his place," he often fumed. He had also said that she would be able to cope since she was to resume night duties soon.

Mr. Enebeli was himself a Kings' College Old Boy. He had always insisted that Gabriel must attend the same school. He wasn't admitted in JSS1, so he went on to Valour High. Mr. Enebeli wasn't at ease. It had to be Kings' College; so he followed up the transfer until it finally came through after three years. He usually told Gabriel stories of the food that wasn't anything like home food, the white school uniform with the navy blue blazer and the checkered house wear. He had been in Hyde Johnson's house so he wore the red checkered shirt on navy blue trousers after school hours. He also told him about the dreaded lights out rule. Somehow, Gabriel was looking forward to it, but certainly not the fact that he wouldn't be seeing his mummy everyday.

The Saturday night preceding resumption day, Gabriel almost couldn't sleep all night. He kept thinking about what it would be like to call Harman's House home, who his new friends would be and whether or not he could survive the life at the boarding house. As he lay on his bed, he thought about Racheal, the new girl in his class at Valour High. He was finally beginning to get her attention and then this.

"Biodun will probably have his way now," he soliloquised.

Occasionally, he would stare at his boxes on the

other side of the room. The neatly arranged clothes, white shirts and trousers to one side, green checkered shirts and navy blue trousers to the other. They all had GABRIEL ENEBELI boldly sewn on their hems. And then the next box – his provisions. He had to get up to see this one. He would be going with four sets. His eyes scanned through again; Cornflakes, Milk, Rice Krispies, Golden Morn, Milo, Sugar, Jam, Groundnuts, Butter…those he could immediately see on top. This was the exciting part for him. He moved over to the box of textbooks; some new ones and others that he had used at Valour High, but they all now had his name written on them with a permanent marker.

"Make sure you take good care of them and read them. They cost a lot."

He turned to find his mother standing at the door. She had been watching him.

"Hey mum, I didn't know I left the door open." He got up from his squatting pose. "I'll take care of them."

"Your dad returned with all his books because they didn't steal so much during his time. Thieves were usually expelled from school, but I hear things are different now," she said as she moved towards his bed to sit.

"I'll do my best mum. I'm going to really miss you a lot," he stretched to hug her.

"I'll miss you too, my baby. But remember you are now a big boy. Always remember to read your bible every morning and pray before you do anything else," she was looking straight at him.

"Yes mum. Don't forget you promised to visit me every week."

...

Gabriel could not control the tears that flowed uncontrollably from his eyes down his cheeks, mixing with the drops of rain splattering through the window of the dormitory. He couldn't say for sure why he was crying. Was it the fact that he couldn't get a bed space or the rain that was gaining access through the window to the floor where he had put his mattress to pass the night? Or could it be the reality of the fact that there would be no mummy to check on him tonight. Occasionally, he would think that being in SS2, he should be able to take care of himself but he just couldn't find the courage he knew he needed to face this new reality. Then he thought of Racheal. What would she think of him if she found him this way, crying like a baby? "No, this is not right," he thought. He tried to brace up. He thought of dad, then mum, when she would visit. Then slowly, he began to fall asleep amidst the rain drops.

Emmanuel was the first friend Gabriel had in school. He was the one who succeeded in talking him out of his misery and helped him acclimatise with life as a 'boarder'. He was the one who replaced a mattress belonging to an SS1 student above him on the double bunk with that of Gabriel the day after he resumed.

"See, you're a senior boy. Only SS3 boys are your seniors here and they don't have our time because they have *waheck* to write. You can command any junior boy to do anything for you," Emmanuel had heartened him.

Those words sounded very strange to Gabriel. 'Command…to do anything'. He couldn't contain them. So, while Emmanuel would sight a gathering of SS1 students and shout, "A boy! Last boy!" and all the students would come running to him, he would stand in amazement and watch as Emmanuel would usually throw both their buckets to the student who arrived last and say, "Get me two buckets of water. I need them under my bed in two minutes."

When would he have the courage to do that? He would think to himself. It felt like he would be acting unfairly to ask a junior student to fetch him water, iron his clothes or wash them, when he could do it himself. After all, they had their own lives to live too.

"It is because you were not a boarder when you were a junior boy, if not, you would also be wicked." Emmanuel would say, anytime he talked about his thoughts about 'commanding' the junior students. He would spend sometime thinking about the word 'wicked'. He never wanted to be that, whatever it meant.

'Lights out' was perhaps the most strictly observed

rule Gabriel had noticed since the beginning of the week, just like his dad had told him. Once the siren went off at 10:30pm, all lights in the school went out and everyone was expected to either be in bed or be on the way there as quickly as possible. The senior boarding house master, Mr. Effiong, and other house masters would usually go on patrol to ensure absolute compliance. So, Gabriel was extremely surprised when Emmanuel told him after lunch that Friday about a certain plan they would execute after lights out.

"We are going somewhere tonight," Emmanuel said clutching his fork and knife.

"Going somewhere? When did you get an exeat?"

"We are not using exeats; we are going to have fun with some friends at the beach," Emmanuel reiterated, wearing a broad smile.

Gabriel pleaded to be left out of the plan. He felt let down by the thought of Emmanuel being one of those students his dad had told him about; those who 'scale the fence' to go out at night. He was determined not to have anything to do with Emmanuel anymore from that moment on. He would seek out a new bed space and consider being friends with Leke, the short boy who had been hanging around his locker to beg for either sugar or milk since he resumed. Leke looked like a decent student. He always had his keys hung around his neck and was always with his bible, even in class. He thought about asking him about the Kings' College Christian Fellowship on Sunday, hoping that would start a friendship.

"So, you don't want to go. *You go miss oh*. You need to see the kind of big chics we roll with at the beach," Emmanuel was still hoping to persuade him.

"This guy just doesn't get it," Gabriel thought. He had never been into 'chics', not to mention the 'big' ones. He wasn't interested and he had to get this across as simply as possible.

"See, Emma, let me tell you something, I am not into those things and I will really appreciate it if you just let me be," he said finally.

"Is that it? No *wahala*, you are on your own." Emmanuel began to walk faster towards the dormitory.

Gabriel took a long stern look at Emmanuel from the rear as he walked away, he thought about this fifteen year old in the midst of 'big girls' on a beach at midnight. He asked himself what they could possibly be doing, and then he tried not to think about it. Instead he thought about the fact that his mum would be visiting tomorrow and that he would be able to tell her how his one week in the boarding house had been. The noise from the students on the basketball court caught his attention. He wondered how come they had started playing so quickly after lunch.

At the dormitory, after the evening prep session, he decided he would try to be awake until after the lights went out to see if Emmanuel was really serious about this plan.

"Have you changed your mind?" Emmanuel got up

from his bed to ask. "I still have some nice *barfs* that will really fit you."

"Emmanuel, are you really serious about this?"

"Stay there and be asking stupid questions." He sat back into his bed and lay on his back.

...

Gabriel woke up at 12:30am. He wasn't happy he had fallen asleep so easily. Perhaps he was too tired. He pulled his mosquito net up to look down on Emmanuel's bed. It was empty. He got down from the bed and began to pace the dormitory quietly. He noticed two other empty beds. Everybody else was asleep except Leke. Gabriel could see the light from his torchlight reflecting on a book. He moved closer to Leke's bed.

"What are you reading by this time?" he whispered quietly.

"Hey, new boy. I'm trying to read my bible," Leke responded. His voice was louder than Gabriel's.

"*Shh*...you will wake guys up." He contemplated asking about Emmanuel's whereabout for a moment and then said, "Do you know where Emmanuel is?" His whisper was even more silent now.

"Emma? Didn't he tell you anything?" Leke's voice was still loud.

"Keep your voice down. He didn't tell me anything.

Two other boys are not in bed."

"They went to *Kay Bee*," Leke was whispering now.

"Where is that? A beach?"

"Yes. Kuramo Beach."

"To do what?"

"To do water and garri. Ask your friend when he comes back," Leke turned off his torchlight. "Please I want to sleep now."

Gabriel thought about saying Emmanuel wasn't his friend. Afterall, it's been less than six days. He chose instead to be a little dramatic. "You want to sleep now right? Me, water and garri…just don't come and beg me for my sugar and milk tomorrow." He walked away quietly, pretending he didn't hear Leke's whispers trying to call him back.

Mrs. Enebeli arrived at about 12:00 noon later that day. It was Emmanuel who came to call Gabriel from the field. He was walking past the car park when Mrs. Enebeli called him and asked if he knew "Gabriel Enebeli in SS2, Harman's House."

"He is my friend ma."

"Oh, thank God. Please call him for me, tell him his mum is here. Meanwhile, your trouser is falling."

Emmanuel smiled. "It is not falling ma, that's how it is." He walked faster to try to seek out Gabriel and give him the good news, "They've come for you!"

Gabriel couldn't wait to get to the car park. He was

sure there would be a good meal at last, after a week of eating what he had concluded was tasteless food. They talked about almost everything – home, dad, his former school, his new school. He thought of telling her about Emmanuel but he knew what she would say and he was already doing that.

After his mum left, he thought of confronting Emmanuel, but he decided against it. It wasn't his business really, and Leke was going to be his friend now. That afternoon, he ordered the junior boy next to Leke's bed to take his place above Emmanuel.

On Monday, Emmanuel asked why he decided to change his bed. Gabriel didn't have anything to say, but he remembered complaining about the spring on the bed. Emmanuel did not look convinced. He had directed his anger towards the junior boy, "If you bed-wet, I'll finish you!" before talking to Gabriel moments after. "Anyway, you really missed out on Friday. You needed to have seen the chics that came to *Kay Bee* that day. There's no way you wouldn't have had one; at least you still have your pocket money," he said scornfully.

Gabriel was quiet. He didn't know exactly how to respond, so he simply remained quiet. He couldn't understand what was getting Emmanuel excited after they had all seen two students flogged during the Assembly that morning for being caught up after lights out. Emmanuel went on and on about how much fun he had on the beach with the other guys from school. They were twelve in all that night. Suddenly Emmanuel seemed to have remembered something.

"Yes! I almost forgot!" he said excitedly, "we met a chic that knows you."

"Knows me?" Gabriel hissed.

"I'm serious *oh*…what's that her name again *oh*?" Emmanuel was looking up seriously. Gabriel started to walk away. "Do you think I'm joking? Wait! Yes…Racheal! Her name is Racheal," he shouted excitedly.

Gabriel turned back. He couldn't believe his ears. "Racheal?" This couldn't be a joke because he had never mentioned her to anyone here. She only showed up in his thoughts and dreams. "How can you say you met Racheal at the beach at night?" He looked distressed suddenly.

"Oh, so you know her?"

"How did you come to know that she knows me?"

"She heard that we are *Kay Cee* boys now?"

"So?"

"She just asked if we knew one Gabriel that just transferred to *Kay Cee* and I said I know you."

"So, how am I sure it's the Racheal I know, there could be another Gabriel that just transferred."

"She is a Valour High chic; she's fine like this, fair, tall, slim…"

"It's okay, it's okay." Gabriel didn't know what to say. "My God! Racheal? I can't believe this." He was leaning on the pole of the walk way. He felt like sitting.

"Oh oh, is she your babe or what?"

"No, yes…as in, I know her."

"I know you know her; I'm asking if she is your babe because *the chic set die.* If she is your babe or you have any plans, it is better you follow us there and talk to her *oh*, if not, somebody else will just snatch your babe. She was even with one dude from YSL all night."

Emmanuel noticed that Gabriel looked lost. "Don't just stand there looking, make up your mind once and for all. From the way you are looking, she is either your babe or you have mega plans. So, act up, lover boy!"

Gabriel turned and started to walk away again. Emmanuel didn't stop talking. "I am just saying my own. *If you like vex, na you sabi. You too dey vex sef.*"

Gabriel couldn't concentrate on anything else throughout the week. He couldn't wait till Friday to be able to go see if the girl in question was truly Racheal. He asked Emmanuel if they had to wait till Friday and he had told him that they only go there in droves on Fridays; the other days were usually not as exciting because Racheal and the other girls may not come.

That Friday, Emmanuel gave him a red polo shirt and a pair of black jeans to wear. He thought about telling Leke what he was about to do but thought that he would need to justify it and he just wasn't ready for that. He promised himself that he wouldn't stay long at the beach.

He wouldn't even wait for the other guys. He simply needed to see Racheal for himself.

As he landed on the other side of the fence, Gabriel felt like a thief. He felt like going over the fence again and back to his bed. But the thought of Racheal being on the beach with some guy strengthened his guts. He simply could not stand the thought. He looked at his wrist watch; it was quarter past midnight. He froze.

"*Wetin dey do your guy? Why him dey look like mumu?*" Umar was talking to Emmanuel. Gabriel was slowing them down.

Emmanuel turned to Gabriel. "*Wetin dey happen? You dey fear?*"

"*I tell you say make you no bring this small boy come with us,*" Debo, who completed the quartet, was trying to wave down a taxi.

"I am not a small boy!" Gabriel couldn't believe he was shouting.

"Then prove it and let's get out of here!" Debo screamed back.

"Guys, we might need to arrange bike *oh, no cab wan stop,*" Emmanuel tried to change the subject.

They walked across the road to Law School junction. They made jokes about three prostitutes they saw on the other side, waiting for potential customers. After about five minutes, they found two bikes that were willing to take them to Kuramo Beach, at exorbitant prices.

...

Umar was the first to hear the gun shots as they approached Ahmadu Bello Way. He was seating behind Deji on one bike. He could also hear siren blaring from a distance. Emmanuel and Gabriel were on the other bike, about seventy metres ahead of them.

"*Wetin be that?*" he asked Deji.

"*Wetin?*"

"*You no hear?*" The gunshots were sounding louder and closer.

"*O boy, gun o!*" The bike rider halted abruptly. A black SUV zoomed out from the road on the left, swaying to the right and then to the left. Two gun wielding masked men were seating on the windows of the back seats, guns pointing backwards, shooting sporadically. As the SUV joined the road, the three of them – Deji, Umar, the bike rider and his bike - went flat on the ground, facing the bar beach.

Soon a police van came out through the same road; their shots were targeted at the SUV. Emmanuel and Gabriel were just trying to get off their bike. Gabriel fell off the bike, landed on his back, face towards the sky. Emmanuel got down to face the ground too while the bike rider fell with his bike.

Later, after the vehicles had gone and they could no longer hear the sounds of shooting and siren blaring. Umar whispered something about getting up to Deji. He wasn't too sure. The bike rider got up.

"Lazy men, see them," he cackled.

Deji and Umar jumped up. Umar spoke first.

"O'boy, that was very close." Deji didn't respond. He tried to dust himself up.

Suddenly, they heard Emmanuel's voice from the distance. They quickly got on the bike to meet him in front. There was blood on the floor.

"Jeees!" Deji shouted as he got down. "*Wetin happen?*"

Gabriel was still on the floor, blood sodden on his back.

"*E be like say bullet hit am,*" Emmanuel responded.

"*Yawa! Na yawa be this o,*" Umar bent to look at Gabriel. "*O boy, wetin happen now?*" Gabriel gestured to his back, he couldn't talk.

"*Omo, make we no stay here dey ask question oh,* lets get this guy to the hospital," Emmanuel reasoned. A car zoomed past them at break-neck speed.

"*You get police report wey you go show for hospital? This is gunshot oh!*" Umar had one hand on his head and the other at his back.

"*So, make we just stay here dey look abi?*" He picked Gabriel by the right hand; Deji looked at the others and then picked him by the left. They placed him on the bike behind the rider and Emmanuel sat behind him. "*Make una climb the second bike come oh,"* he instructed.

"*Where we dey go?*" the bike rider asked.

"Hospital!"

"Which one?"

"Anyone!"

"*No be anyone oga. This one na gun. No be any hospital dey cure gun.*"

"St. Nicholas!" That was the only hospital he could remember, it was not far from the Main Campus on Lagos Island, where they had been from JSS1 to JSS3. He knew they performed surgeries so he reasoned they should be able to deal with a gunshot wound.

"*That one na after Obalende oh. Your money na one thousand.*"

"Just go!"

"Help! Please help us!" Emmanuel was shouting as he ran into the ground floor of St. Nicholas Hospital. "My friend is dying, please help us!" The nurse at the reception quickly ran into an adjacent room, and then ran out about a minute later with another nurse carrying a stretcher.

"Please ma, we have an emergency!" The nurse informed Mrs. Enebeli as she entered her office on the first floor.

"What sort of emergency is that, Nurse Kike?" she was looking through a file on her table.

"It's a gunshot ma!"

"What!" she stood. "Do they have police report?" she asked as she quickly made for the door with Nurse Kike.

"I don't think so ma. I think they are students."

"Jesus! They?"

"No ma. Only one was shot, but his friends brought him."

They were at the ground floor now.

"Were you the ones that brought the shot student?" Mrs. Enebeli asked Umar, Deji and Emmanuel at the reception.

"Yes ma," they chorused.

"Are you sure you were not shot too?" she pointed to Emmanuel. He had blood all over his shirt. He shook his head in disapproval. "I will go and attend to the boy, but we will need a police report. Is that okay?" The three of them nodded. "Do I know you?" she asked, pointing to Emmanuel again. He shook his head vigorously. He was shaking. He recognised her from the visiting day.

"Doctor! Doctor!" Nurse Kike was shouting with her head stuck out from the emergency room. "The boy has stopped breathing."

Mrs. Enebeli ran into the emergency room.

Thunder from the gods

I SAT ON THE BACK OF THE OLD LORRY. I wasn't alone: Me. Mattresses. Pots. Chairs. Kegs of water. My fellow corps members. Etcetera. My heart skipped each time the lorry emerged from another pot-hole. It skipped not just for fear of falling off the old lorry which must have been manufactured before my parents met, but because my expectations were high. I quickly bent my head to avoid one of the long tree branches sticking out to the dusty, rarely travelled road.

The lorry was taking us to Obosima; a village in Ohaji/Egbema local government area of Imo State. We were going there to fulfil a prophecy, one I didn't even know about before then. I had not exactly joined this group of God-loving, tongue-talking, demon-chasing young Christians, but I couldn't resist the prospect of having a story, perhaps a cover, to present to my editor the following week. They called it 'Rural Rugged Evangelism'. It had to be a good story.

I was an undergraduate the first time I heard those three words. To be honest, I was scared when I did. The first one – rural – was bad enough. The second – rugged – was worse. The third – evangelism – had always made my heart skip. Each time I heard that last one, I remembered the experience with a certain man one Sunday afternoon in 2005. I had followed Pastor Durotoluwa and the other members of the evangelism unit of my local church to evangelise. I was paired with Sister Shade. I thought she was a 'hotter' Christian than me. That was until she said something about the Trinity that provoked the man we were trying to preach to. "Don't tell me that! Am I a baby? Three different people and they are still one person? Am I a fool?" He removed his glasses. "Please leave my house; I don't have time for this. Leave. Now!" I wish I had heard exactly what Sister Shade had said that angered the man. But I wasn't listening. I was too focused on the books on the shelf behind the man whose soul we were trying to win to God.

I was told about how 'corpers' gave their time, energy and money to preach the gospel in several rural communities around the country. I had instantly wanted to be part of it one day. Not the evangelism but everything else. That day had arrived, but I was only there to do my job, with my pen, paper, a tape recorder, a camera and my five senses.

We reached a police check-point and the others began to laugh and shout, "Ajuwaya," "Ahoha," as the lorry staggered past. I noticed the name tag on one of the police uniforms – ISMAILA D. A. He must have been from the north. We bumped slowly past another pot-hole. The lorry shook.

***

We were the first set of travellers to arrive at the camp site. That is apart from the executives who had been there for three days already. They had been fasting and praying for the success of the weekend long spiritual exercise. They had been preparing the place for our arrival.

He looked really rough, the one they all called 'Prayo'. He was very slim and very tall. He had bathroom slippers on and looked like he had not truly eaten good food in three days. The other one that came behind him was the one they called 'Rugged'. That was his official name and he looked just like that. He had tribal marks and said "hall" instead of 'all'. He asked the sisters if they brought "heggs."

His trousers were folded just below his knees and his leather slippers looked like something from an ancient movie. He had a t-shirt on. I read the words, 'One big family' to myself. "I love this family of God...so closely knitted into one..." he hummed as he walked past me to help with the luggage from the lorry. I was not disposed.

We set out to prepare temporary hostels in one of the classrooms; they had been marked 'Abrahams' and 'Sarahs' at two separate ends of the corridor. The sisters began to select the clothed mattresses.

"*Ah*, Sarahs, why are you doing this *ke*?" It was Rugged, the one with the tribal marks.

"Don't mind them sir, they prefer we sleep on the floor," one of the brothers remarked.

I tried to concentrate on writing my details in the registration log. I omitted the 'Zone' and 'Department' columns in the form. I didn't belong to any. I heard the sound of buses in the distance. More people had arrived. I quickly dropped the pen and hurried towards the mattresses, picked one and followed the short brother in front of me. I dropped the mattress in a corner of the room, placed my bag on it and walked back towards the door. The mattresses outside had vanished. I was sure we wouldn't need to worry. At least until it was time to sleep.

My legs ached after we went on the march round the community. They had to know we had arrived. There would be a film show, we told them. Jesus would deliver them from all oppression of the devil. I also returned with images of sacrificial offerings – Coca-cola and bread – placed at ugly looking shrines in some houses we passed. I kept singing one of the songs we sang on the way back, "*Nma nma diri gi, chineke, Nma nma diri gi, onye oma.*" I didn't know the meaning.

***

It was a long night after that. The villagers gathered in their numbers from God knows where. Men, women and children. The latter duo were more. It hadn't seemed like they were so many when we marched round the village a few hours before.

"God is determined to set this village free! This is your hour of deliverance. Come out now if you want to receive Jesus Christ as your lord and saviour." The president, who we called "Papa," bellowed after a long sermon. The villagers started to hurry to the front. I wondered if they heard him correctly. He didn't share my sentiments, "Oh thank you father. To you alone be all the glory!" he screamed at the top of his voice.

"Do these people really understand what they are coming out for, or do they just want to catch a glimpse of the preacher? Do they know that this would mean that they would need to forsake their traditions and old ways of life, possibly burn their ancient family shrines along with the gods that ate bread and drank Coca-cola?" Just then, Papa's words interrupted my thoughts, he seemed to have heard what I was thinking.

"Thank you father…there are some of you here who have shrines, God wants you to burn them down. We will go with you to burn them down. Come to my right hand side if you are like that here."

My heart began to beat faster; I wasn't expecting that and I would certainly not be a part of the shrine burning adventure. No one came to the right. He repeated the instruction and then, one man moved to the right. Another followed. Then another. Then another.

"Oh thank you father. You are ever faithful." Papa wiped his forehead with his hands. "Don't be afraid, the devil can't do anything to you."

By the time the night was finally over around 11pm, there was joy in not a few hearts. Not just because the night had been a huge success, but because of the massive response to the call for salvation by the people of Obosima. For many 'Jesus Corpers', that was their reward for all the sacrifices. For travelling several miles; for giving their one month allowance to the course; for leaving their more convenient abodes in better parts of the state. And then I remembered the many that would not get a place to sleep.

With that in mind, I hurried through my meal of

garri and egusi soup and before long, I was in bed. Not sleeping, I was thinking. "What could make 'corpers' go through these sacrifices? How did this whole idea come to be? What would happen at the end of this?"

In the midst of my thoughts, there was an argument somewhere in the hall about who was first to a certain mat and another fellow had refused to allow a third person on his. Then it occurred to me that the 'Sarahs' will also be facing the same challenge, because they appeared to be more than the 'Abrahams'. Well, I was lucky to be sleeping on a mattress then, even though it was a very torn one.

The next morning, I decided to find answers to some of my questions; after all, I was there to do my job and should not get carried away. So, immediately after the joint morning devotion and camp instructions, I went after the leaders of the movement.

The General Secretary of the Nigerian Christian Corpers' Fellowship is called 'Uncle'. His real names are Deji Abiona. Put 'Brother' before that. Brother Deji studied Computer Science at the university.

"How did this begin?" I put my journalistic instincts to work.

"*Rural-rugged* is actually a result of a prophecy by the late Pa Elton, who was a missionary to Nigeria. He predicted that 'one day, the Nigerian government would be paying Nigerian youths to preach the gospel.' That was long before the NYSC scheme started. This is the fulfilment of that prophecy," Abiona said.

"So how does the fellowship get corps members to believe so much in this vision causing them to leave their comfort zones?"

I thought his response was a little too saintly: "Left to man, it may be difficult. But it is running on prophetic wings and divine grace, that is why this is happening."

Noted. But I wasn't satisfied. "Is there a practical plan of action in place to get this done?" That is what I set out to ask the fellowship president, or Papa, Brother Fidelis Olubanwo.

"By God's grace, we are building on the foundation laid by past leaders and because of the growth and development the fellowship has witnessed over the years, it is one of the events you look forward to as a Christian Corper and majorly it has been God."

"Another saintly answer," I thought. God is at the centre of everything. But a lot of logistics would also have gone into planning and executing an event of such magnitude. This would usually come with huge costs. But trust clergies, whether 'corpers' or full fledged, they prefer to tell you, "We thank God for everything," than to say exactly how much was spent on the programme.

But my nosy inquiries from the finance department soon revealed later that close to five hundred thousand naira had been expended as at 5pm on Saturday; on feeding, transportation, free cloths given to the villagers, free medical care and drugs, equipment and lighting, generators and more. According to the Financial Director, these monies are generated from the offerings, tithes, pledges and donations of corps members under the NCCF.

"How come the huge budget doesn't seem to reflect in the level of comfort available here?" I asked.

"We were expecting one hundred and fifty people but three hundred and fifty showed up," the finance director answered.

As for comfort level, Papa had also mentioned that, "Here, it is not the comfortable kind of evangelism. It is Rugged because you don't expect convenience. Our mandate is to reach souls for Christ, so you have to look beyond the inconveniences."

That was the one reason I managed not visiting the convenience for three days and two nights. He continued, "We sacrifice our allowances, we leave our comfort zones and so many other sacrifices. That is why it is called Rural Rugged Evangelism."

As the corps members returned in twos later from the 'one on one' evangelism, the smiles on their faces seemed to tell the story. It had been another successful outing with bountiful harvest of converts. This is what seemed to make up for the inconveniences – the lives that are 'saved' through their efforts. As we prepared for the evening programmes, we had no clue whatsoever that the night would turn out to be more eventful and dramatic than we all could have imagined.

The drama presentation flowed smoothly. It was about the prevalence of the power of God over the power of darkness. But the drama was barely over when I began to feel rain drops on my skin. It felt like mild trickles at first, but two minutes later, the gathering was over. In its place was heavy downpour. We tried hard to rescue the musical equipment from under the sudden intense deluge as the villagers ran in different directions to get shelter from the rain.

The rain continued for three hours, putting paid to any lingering hopes. This was the worst that could happen; surely the meeting was over. But the rain had more plans, or was it the gods?

It was a thundering sound that woke me up from deep slumber. It seemed like a dream, so I managed to continue sleeping. But at 12:41am, the sounds of the announcement over the megaphone finally got me up. What I saw at the ground when I obeyed the call to "Come out and join the prayers" amazed me. There was ongoing fervent prayers; deliverance, prophecies…all kinds of things. I was lost for a few minutes and wondered how I could have been asleep all along. I later got to hear the origin of the gathering.

The thundering sound I had heard was not a dream

after all. It had happened. It had wounded six corps members, I learnt. It had sparked off the prayers.

"I saw myself lifted from the ground in the hostel and I landed outside," said a tall brother I identified from the lorry. He had just removed his phone from the socket at the entrance of the hostel and was going back in with his phone in hand when he heard heavy thundering, preceded by lightning. Even though I initially did not want to believe his story, I could not doubt the bruises on his left hand; I could not also deny the testimony of five others who had sustained various injuries simultaneously from the incident. Another brother they called Mark, was connecting wires from one hostel to another when the thunder struck.

"I couldn't see anything for three minutes. I didn't know when I started crying," he recalled.

But the rains weren't done yet. Only that this time, Jesus Corpers refused to go back indoors. "This is a prayer we cannot stop praying," announced the masculine voice over the battery operated megaphone. He was standing on the corridor, under a shade, safe from the rain. At this time, the wires around the camp were all burnt and the generator had been damaged. This, I thought, was a diabolically intended aspersion on an otherwise exemplary endeavour; hence the determination to keep praying even under the rain.

"This whole thing must have been a spiritual attack. As far as I am concerned, the gods of this land wanted to shed blood, but God took all the glory," I overheard a lady say after the prayers.

Well, I was not prepared to begin to seek proof to such claims that cold Sunday morning but I was just as grateful as everyone else was to God that there were no fatalities. That the three hundred and fifty corps members who registered for the exercise were returning home safely; with joy and a sense of fulfilment. A sense of conquering the gods too.

"This land will never be the same again," said Uncle. "They have seen the light and darkness cannot comprehend it."

As I watched him take my place in the old lorry that was to take us back to Owerri, I managed to grab the last seat in the famous fellowship bus. I had only one thing on my mind. Okay, two things. The passion of these youths for the things of God, and two, the need to use a decent toilet urgently.

Passport Office

THE CHILD BESIDE YOU KEPT TUGGING at his mother's breasts. You tried to get your mind off the boy and his young mother. She must have been barely eighteen. Instead, you concentrated on the officers, walking hurriedly across the long waiting room, greeting one another, some stopping to share a few jokes, their uniforms grumpily ironed. You tried to read some of the names on the uniforms. You thought the one who came back with people's files called out names too loudly.

"Nwosu! Nwosu Henry!" he shouted before stretching his hands as he walked towards the owner of the file. You watched Henry walk up to the officer and filch his file off as if someone or something had upset him.

Then you looked at your wrist-watch and remembered that you had been on the queue, moving slowly from chair to chair towards the photograph capturing room, for more than an hour. That, you thought, was enough to upset anyone.

You wondered what would happen to the files after your international passports had been issued or in your own case, re-issued. Then the child began to yowl. His mother still hadn't done what he wanted. You thought about talking to her to yield to his demands but you were discouraged by her age. It could be considered chary.

Then you noticed that a few people in mufti didn't join the queue, they simply walked through to the door behind an officer and you never saw them again. Just as you tried to reason it out, you heard a man from the top of the queue begin to protest stridently. He had a fulani cap on, but didn't speak with an accent.

"This is not right! This is not right at all. Are we not all human beings? We have been on this line for almost two hours. How will some people just come and go in, just like that? Because they know somebody?"

There was silence in the hall. The officers stood for about a minute, gobsmacked. Then they went on as if nothing had happened. Then another woman beside him offered solidarity.

"It is not fair at all. This is so wrong," she said and hissed several times repeatedly. As soon as she did that, comments began to fly around the hall. You kept quiet. Then you thought about the activities you had observed outside the passport office, touts beckoning with promises of "*sharp sharp* passport;" officers you had seen at the entrance being 'settled' by the clients they were about to assist, but you didn't understand it until now.

Suddenly, the officer who had taken the lady in mufti into the capturing room came back into the hall. He wore a frown. "What is it? Please let's maintain decorum!" His scowl seemed to send the hall into simulated silence. Not the man in the Fulani cap.

"People have been on this queue for hours, yet you keep taking people in illegally," he said and then looked away from the officer.

There was another deafening silence. You thought "illegally" was too strong. Then the officer responded in a bogus baritone, "Better mind your business. This one is *oga* approved *oh!* Order from above."

The sweeping laughter that followed was bizarre, but you also laughed, the man with the Fulani cap laughed. Even the child beside you giggled, probably at his mother's laughter.

Soon, it was your turn to go into the capturing room, and as you confirmed your details to the officer in front of you and had your photograph taken, you eavesdropped on another officer informing the man whose photograph she was capturing that he was going to buy her lunch for her efforts. You hissed impulsively.

"Take your print-out from the printer to the officers outside, they'll attend to you," the officer in front of you said. You thanked him and walked out through the exit where you met two female officers sitting languidly. Their job was to collect your file along with a photocopy of your print-out and ask you to write 'Original copy received by me' on it.

"Drop your form *na!*" the first officer screamed at the young man ahead of you, before handing out lessons on how to behave in a public place to him. "*When you come place like this, look as others dey do and do like that.*" Then she turned to her colleague. "All these your *ngbati* people *sef,*" a debasing allusion to people from the western part of the country. You tried to ignore her as her colleague pointed towards a small kiosk and asked you to go make a photocopy of your print-out.

"*You no fit write?*" the first officer was asking the young man in front of her when you returned.

"*I no school for here. I school for French,*" the young man explained and then pleaded, "please, help me write."

"*Me I no dey write for free o. Na money I dey take write,*" she retorted. You thought you didn't hear her correctly and then she went on. "*Abi you no know how much my parents take send me go school?*"

As you walked out of the premises, you couldn't get your mind off *Oga approved*. You thought about the deep seated corruption in the country's public service. You thought about the girl and the child and it occurred to you that she may not be his mother after all, or why would she have refused to breast-feed him. It mirrored the country's present fate in the hands of her leaders. You looked at the green passport. You tried to stay inspired.

'SEUN SALAMI

A note about the author

'Seun Salami is a writer, an author and editor. He wrote the back page satire column 'Conversations' for *National Standard* between 2007 and 2008. His articles have also appeared in the likes of *The SUN* and *The PUNCH* Newspapers among other platforms. 'Seun is also the Head of Publishing at Bookvine. He holds a BSc in Journalism from the Lagos State University and an MSc in Mass Communication from the University of Lagos. *The Son of your Father's Concubine* is his first work of fiction.

You can follow 'Seun on Twitter/Instagram @SeunWrites

Acknowledgments

Thank you Lord, for the gift and grace. For the effortless wisdom to write and title these stories.

Thanks Mum and Dad, for all the love and support.

Thanks Sanya and Kemi, for being exceptional siblings.

Thanks Dorcas, for always being so caring and supportive. You're virtuous in every sense of the word.

Thanks to everyone who contributed in one way or the other to making this book a reality. I appreciate you all, may God bless you richly.

'SeunWrites
21.08.2011
12:38am